"That **You.**

"How coul

"That was the summer we were getting ready to go into the first grade," he said. "Do you think that was what started our little game of one-upmanship?"

"Maybe." She tried to remember when their rivalry began, but the feel of him stroking her hair distracted her. "I–it's been so long, I'm not really certain when it began or why."

"Me either. But one thing's for sure. You've been driving me nuts for most of my life, Abigail Langley."

Her heart sped up as she met his piercing hazel gaze. "I'm sorry, but you've done your fair share of driving me to the brink, too."

"Don't be sorry." He cupped the back of her head with his hand to gently pull her forward. "There are different kinds of crazy, darlin'." His lips lightly brushed hers. "Right now, I'm thinking that it's the good kind."

* * *

Dear Reader,

One of my favorite things about being an author is
when I'm asked to collaborate with other authors on a
miniseries like the Texas Cattleman's Club. I not only
get to work with some of the most talented authors in
romance, I get to help refine the details that make the
stories compelling and remembered long after the series
ends.

By now, I'm sure you've met Bradford Price and
Abigail Langley. Lifelong competitors, they have been
playing a game of one-upmanship since they were six
years old. But finding themselves in a close race for the
presidency of the Texas Cattleman's Club, the stakes
have never been higher.

I really enjoyed the journey Brad and Abby take as they
learn that sometimes just below the surface of a fierce
rivalry, there's a burning attraction that once surfaced
can't be denied—no matter how hard they try. It is my
fervent hope that you enjoy reading *In Bed with the
Opposition* as much as I enjoyed writing it.

All the best,

Kathie DeNosky

KATHIE DeNOSKY

IN BED WITH THE OPPOSITION

Special thanks and acknowledgment to Kathie DeNosky
for her contribution to the
Texas Cattleman's Club: The Showdown miniseries.

ISBN-13: 978-0-373-73139-8

IN BED WITH THE OPPOSITION

Recycling programs
for this product may
not exist in your area.

KATHIE DeNOSKY

lives in her native southern Illinois with her big, lovable Bernese mountain dog, Nemo. Writing highly sensual stories with a generous amount of humor, Kathie's books have appeared on the *USA TODAY* bestseller list and received a Write Touch Readers Award and a National Readers' Choice Award. Kathie enjoys going to rodeos, traveling to research settings for her books and listening to country music. Readers may contact Kathie at P.O. Box 2064, Herrin, Illinois 62948-5264 or email her at kathie@kathiedenosky.com. They can also visit her website, www.kathiedenosky.com.

This book is dedicated to the wonderful authors
I worked with on this miniseries. You all are amazing!

And to Charles Griemsman. It's been a real treat and
I look forward to working on many more projects together.

* * *

Don't miss a single book in this series!

Texas Cattleman's Club: The Showdown
*They are rich and powerful, hot and wild.
For these Texans, it's showdown time!*

One

Brad Price stared at the object in his hand, then at the tiny baby girl grinning up at him as she grabbed her foot and tried to stuff her tiny toes into her mouth. When had Sunnie lost her little pink sock?

Scratching his head, he scanned the floor. She had it on when they arrived at the Texas Cattleman's Club not two minutes ago. How could a baby barely six months old be so quick?

He once again glanced at the disposable diaper he held. What in the name of all that was holy had he gotten himself into, taking on the responsibility of raising his late brother's child? He knew about as much when it came to taking care of a baby as he did about piloting a spacecraft to the moon.

When he had made the decision to adopt Sunnie, he had even gone so far as to give serious consideration to dropping out of the race for the TCC presidency. But only briefly. He had made a commitment to seek the office, and he never went back on his word. Besides, he believed in the club and everything it stood for, and he intended to raise Sunnie to believe in those values, too.

The organization needed someone with a level head and a solid plan, and he was the man with both. He had several ideas on ways to bridge the ever-widening gap between the old guard and the younger members in order to unite the club and renew the solidarity that had always been an integral part of the TCC. It was something that had to be done to ensure its future and to continue the valuable services it had always provided for the residents of Royal, Texas.

But if he didn't figure out how to change Sunnie's diaper, and damned quick, it would all be a moot point. He would miss outlining his vision for the TCC at the annual general meeting, and for the first time in the club's history, a woman—the only woman ever to be allowed to join the organization—would be voted into office by default. He'd be damned if he'd let that happen.

Closing his eyes, Brad counted to ten. He could do this. He had a master's degree in financial planning, had graduated from the University of Texas summa cum laude and in the years since had built a thriving career as a certified financial planner, amassing a sizable fortune of his own. Surely he could figure out something as simple as changing a baby's disposable diaper.

But where did he start? And once he figured out

how to get the one she was wearing off and the new one in position, how the hell was he supposed to fasten it around her waist?

As he studied the sides of the diaper Sunnie was wearing, he tried to remember what his housekeeper, Juanita, had told him when she gave him a detailed lecture on diaper changing before she left him high and dry to rush off to Dallas for the birth of her third grandchild. Unfortunately, he had been preoccupied with putting the final touches on the campaign wrap-up speech he was supposed to give at today's meeting and barely heard the woman. In hindsight, he should have taken extensive notes or at the very least given the matter his undivided attention.

Just when he decided he was going to have to find one of the club's female employees and ask her to do the honors of changing his niece, he heard the door of the coat room open. "Thank God," he muttered, hoping it was someone who knew more about the intricacies of a disposable diaper than he did. "Would you mind giving me a hand here?"

"Having a bit of a problem, Mr. Price?" a familiar female voice asked. Relieved that help had arrived, Brad couldn't work up the slightest bit of irritation at the obvious humor in Abigail Langley's tone.

Turning to find his lifelong nemesis standing just inside the door, a knowing smile curving her full coral lips, Brad released a frustrated breath. They had been rivals for as long as he could remember and for the past several months bitter opponents for the coveted office of president of the TCC. At any other time her perceptive expression would have no doubt had him grinding his teeth. At the moment, he couldn't feel anything but gratitude.

"How are you at putting these things on a baby?" he asked, holding up the offending object.

Laughing, Abby hung up her coat. "Don't tell me the mighty Bradford Price has run into a problem he can't solve with his superior logic."

Not at all surprised that she took the opportunity to make fun of him, he gave her a sarcastic smile. "Cute, Langley. Now will you get over here and help me out?"

She walked over to stand beside the plush sofa, where his niece lay nibbling on her toes as she stared happily up at them. "You don't have the slightest clue what you're doing, do you, Bradford?"

Her use of his given name never failed to cause a slow burn deep in his gut. He knew she was using it to taunt him, much as she had done when they were in school. But he couldn't afford to retaliate. If he did she might not help him, and there was no point in denying the obvious anyway. They both knew he was in way over his head. Besides, arguing with her wouldn't get him any closer to getting the damned diaper changed.

"Isn't it apparent?" The familiar irritation he always felt when they were together had replaced his earlier relief at seeing her. "Now, are you going to help me or am I going to have to go in search of someone who will?"

"Of course I'll change Sunnie," she said, as she set down her purse and seated herself on the couch beside the baby. "But I'm not doing it to help you." She tickled the baby's rounded little tummy. "I'm doing it for this little angel."

"Fine. Whatever."

He didn't care who Abby was doing it for, as long as his niece was changed and dry in time for him to make arrangements for someone to watch her while he gave his closing campaign speech to the TCC general membership. Then, when all of the candidates had finished speaking and were asked to leave the room for final comments from the members, he fully intended to take Sunnie home for a much-needed nap for both of them.

The day had barely begun and he was already exhausted. Taking care of a baby was proving to be a lot more work than he had anticipated. Aside from the feedings at the most god-awful hours of the day and night, there was so much to take along when they left the house, it was like moving.

"Why didn't you leave the baby with your housekeeper?" Abby asked as she tucked her long, dark red hair behind her ears and reached for the diaper bag Juanita had packed before leaving on her trip.

"She got a call early this morning that her youngest daughter has been scheduled to have a Caesarian delivery tomorrow. She's on her way up to Dallas to be there for the birth," he answered, absently. "She won't be back for a couple of weeks."

Fascinated by Abby's efficiency, he watched her line up baby wipes and powder, then lift Sunnie to place a white pad with pink bunnies on it beneath her. How did women automatically know what to do? Were women born with an extra gene that men didn't have?

That had to be the reason, he decided. He and Abby were the same age, and up until Sunnie came into his life they had both been childless. Yet taking care of a baby seemed to come as naturally to Abby as drawing her next breath, while he was at a loss as to what he should do about everything.

In what Brad would judge to be record time, Abby had the old diaper off of Sunnie and the new one in place. "These are what you use to fasten the diaper around her." She pointed to the tabs on the sides he hadn't noticed before. "They are a softer version of Velcro so as not to scratch her tender skin. All you have to do is make sure it's snug, but not too tight, then—"

Fascinated by the sound of her melodic voice and wondering why he suddenly found it so enchanting, it took a moment for Brad to realize Abby had stopped speaking. "What?"

"Pay attention, Price. You can't be assured that someone will always be around to come to your rescue whenever Sunnie needs changing."

"I am paying attention." He had been listening—just not to the crash course on diapering a baby that Abby had been delivering. He wisely kept that bit of information to himself.

Looking doubtful, she asked, "What did I just tell you?"

Abby had to have the bluest eyes in Texas, he decided as she stared up at him expectantly. They were the color of the blue bonnets that grew wild in the spring, and Brad couldn't help but wonder why he'd never before noticed how vibrant and expressive they were.

"Well, Mr. Price?" The diaper successfully changed,

she picked up Sunnie and stood to face him. "Your niece and I are waiting."

He cleared his throat as he tried to remember what she had said. But the sight of her holding Sunnie, tenderly pressing her lips to the baby's soft cheek, was one Brad didn't think he would ever forget, and he couldn't for the life of him think of one single reason why he found it so compelling.

"Uh…well…let's see."

What the hell was wrong with him? Why all of a sudden was he having trouble concentrating? And why did his lapse of attention have to happen in front of *her*?

He never had problems focusing on a conversation. Why then, couldn't he think of anything but how perfectly shaped Abby's lips were and how soft they would feel on his skin?

"Get it snug. Fasten with Velcro. Avoid pinching tender skin," he finally managed with no small effort.

"Got it." He gave himself a mental pat on the back for at least remembering that much.

"It took you that long to remember something this simple?" she asked, giving him an accusatory look.

"Lucky guess."

"Yup." He shrugged. "But it doesn't matter. The important thing is that I got it right."

She shook her head. "You have to do better than that, Bradford. You can't just guess. You have to learn how to do these things for her." Abby slowly swayed side to side the way he'd seen many women do when they held a baby. "You're her daddy now. You've got to step up to the plate and hit a home run on this. Sunnie is depending on you to know exactly what you're doing and to do it when it needs to be done."

Abby was right. At times he found the responsibility of adopting his late brother's child and raising her as his own to be overwhelming. "Let me assure you, I'll do whatever it takes to see that Sunnie has the best of everything, including the care she needs," he said, irritated that she thought he would do anything less. "I think you know me well enough to realize that I never do anything halfway. When I commit to something, I'll see it through or die trying."

Staring at him a moment, she finally nodded. "Be sure that you do."

They both fell silent when Sunnie laid her little head on Abby's shoulder. It was obvious she was about to go to sleep.

As he watched, Abby closed her eyes and cuddled the baby close. "Don't ever lose sight of how blessed you are to have her in your life, Brad."

"Never." Something about her heartfelt statement and the fact that she had used the preferred variation of his name caught him off guard and without thinking he reached up to lightly run the back of his knuckles along her smooth cheek. "You're going to be a great mom someday, Abigail Langley."

When she opened her eyes, he wasn't prepared for the haunted look that clouded Abby's crystalline gaze. "I'm so sorry, Abby." He could have kicked himself for being so insensitive. It had barely been a year since her husband, Richard, passed away and Brad knew for a fact that they had being trying to start a family when the man died. "I'm sure that one day you'll have a family of your own."

She shook her head. "I wish that were true, but um…" She paused to take a deep breath. "…I'm afraid children aren't in my future."

The resigned tone in her voice had him nodding. "Of course they are. There will be plenty of time for you to have kids. You're only thirty-two, the same as me, and even if you don't meet another man you want to spend the rest of your life with, there are a lot of women choosing single motherhood these days."

She was silent a moment before she spoke again. "It's more complicated than meeting someone or choosing to be a single mother."

"Maybe it seems that way now, but I'm sure later on you'll feel differently," he insisted.

When she looked up at him, a single tear slowly slid down her smooth cheek. "It won't make a difference no matter how much time passes."

He couldn't understand her abject resignation. "What's wrong, Abby?"

She stared at him for several long seconds before she answered. "I'm…not able to have…children."

It was the last thing he expected her to say, and it made him feel like a complete jerk for pressing the issue. "I'm really sorry, Abby. I wasn't aware…" His voice trailed off. What could he say that wouldn't make matters worse?

She shrugged one slender shoulder. "It's not like I haven't known about it for a while. The test results came back the week after Richard's funeral."

That had been a little over a year ago, and Brad

could tell she still struggled with the gravity of it all. Why wouldn't she? To lose your husband and within days learn that you could never have a child? That had to be devastating.

Not wanting to cause her further emotional pain by saying the wrong thing, he decided it would be best not to lend his support with words. He had already put his foot in his mouth once and wanted to avoid doing so again. Putting his arms around her and his sleeping niece, he simply stood there and held her.

But the comforting gesture quickly reminded him of another time when he would have given anything to have her slender body pressed to his. They had just started high school, and over the summer between middle school and freshman year, he had developed more hormones than good sense. At fifteen, he had been more than ready to abandon their rivalry in favor of being able to call her his girlfriend.

Unfortunately, Richard Langley had caught her attention about that time, and from then on it had been obvious that Abby and Richard were destined to be together. And it was just as well, Brad decided. She could push his buttons faster than any female he had ever met and have him grinding his teeth in two seconds flat. It had been that way back then and it was still, after all these years, that way now.

"It would probably be a good idea if we head toward the assembly room," she said, effectively ending his trip down memory lane. "It's almost time for the meeting to be called to order." Her tone was soft, but her voice was steadier than it had been earlier, and he knew she had regained the majority of her composure.

Nodding, Brad released her and took a step back. He wasn't sure what to say that wouldn't make the moment more awkward than it already was. "I should have just enough time to get one of the staff to watch Sunnie before the speeches begin," he finally said, checking his watch.

"How long do you think she'll nap?" Abby asked, walking over to carefully place the infant in the car-seat carrier. "If you think she'll sleep through the speeches, I'll watch her while you address the general membership."

Since Sunnie had come into his life, they had established a truce of sorts, but old habits died hard. He didn't believe for a minute Abby was willingly helping him to win the office they both sought. But neither did he believe she would do something underhanded like wake the baby in the middle of his speech. In all of their years of competing against each other, neither of them had ever resorted to sabotage to come out on top.

"You don't mind?"

"Not at all." She put the baby wipes and powder back into the diaper bag. "But don't think I'm doing it to help you with this election or that I won't take great pleasure in beating the socks off of you when the results are announced at the Christmas Ball."

More comfortable with the return of the rivalry they'd shared for as long as he could remember, he smiled. "Of course not. You're doing it for—"

"Sunnie," she said, picking up her purse and the diaper bag.

Grinning, Brad took hold of the baby carrier's

handle, then put his hand to the small of Abby's back to guide her toward the coat room door. "Ready to go in there and listen to the best wrap-up speech you've ever heard?"

"In your dreams, Price," she said, preceding him out the door and into the hall. "I know you've always been a windbag, but you would have to produce a Texas tornado to impress me."

Walking toward the assembly room, he laughed. "Then you had better prepare yourself, Ms. Langley, because you're about to be blown away."

Seated at the table with all of the candidates running for the various club offices, Abby checked on Sunnie napping peacefully in the baby carrier on the chair between her and Brad. Satisfied the infant would sleep through at least the majority of the speeches, Abby looked around the assembly of Texas Cattleman's Club members.

Up until seven months ago, the TCC had been an exclusively male organization with no thoughts to making it open to women. But she had broken through the glass ceiling and become the first female member in the club's long history.

Unfortunately, the invitation to join had not been because of what she could bring to the club, but due to her last name. Founded by her late husband's great-great-great grandfather, Tex Langley, over a hundred years ago, the TCC had always boasted a member of the Langley family in its ranks. But with Richard's death a year ago, it had been the first time since the organization's inception that a Langley had not been listed on the club's membership roster. She had a little known bylaw requiring Langley representation within the club to thank for her admittance.

She sighed, then squared her shoulders and sat up a little straighter. It didn't matter what the reason was that had gained her membership in the TCC; she'd blazed a trail. Now she fully intended to see that other women were considered for entry into the prestigious ranks just as soon as she became the new club president. She couldn't think of a more fitting way to open the new clubhouse she was sure the members were going to vote to build than to have a membership roster with the names of many of the women who had supported the Texas Cattleman's Club throughout the years.

When her name was announced as the next speaker, she checked on Sunnie one last time before walking up to the podium to outline her agenda. Looking out over the room, she could tell that the older members were less than pleased to have her in their ranks, let alone see her running for the high office. But that was just too bad. It was time they joined the twenty-first century and realized that a woman was just as capable of getting things accomplished as any man.

After going over each point in her plan for the future of the TCC, she ended her speech with a mention of her pet project. "The building committee has hired an architect and presented his plans for a new clubhouse. It is my sincere hope that you vote to move forward with this project to build a new home for our club and the exciting new era we are entering into. In closing, I ask that you all consider what I've said here today and base your vote on what I can bring to the Texas Cattleman's Club presidency, not on my gender or my last name. Thank you, and I look forward to serving as the next president of the Texas Cattleman's Club." As she walked back to the table to take her seat, she received a rousing ovation from some of the club's newer members and a grudging nod of respect from a couple of the older ones.

She was confident that she had done all she could do and represented the Langleys, as well as her gender, to the best of her ability. Now it would be up to the members to decide what direction they wanted the TCC to take when the actual voting took place tomorrow.

"Top that, Price," she said, throwing down a challenge to her lifelong rival.

His hazel eyes twinkled as he rose to his feet and prepared to walk up to the front of the room. "Piece of cake, darlin'."

She wasn't fooled by his use of the endearment. Like most Texas men, Bradford Price called all women "darlin'." What she couldn't understand was why it sent a tiny little shiver coursing throughout her body.

Deciding it was best to ignore her reaction, she concentrated on Brad delivering his speech. She had to admit he was an engaging speaker and had a lot of good ideas—some of them paralleling her own. But that didn't mean she was ready to concede.

For as long as she could remember she and Brad Price had been pitted against each other in one competition or another. Sometimes he won, other times she came out on top. But the rivalry was ever present and at times quite fierce.

Abby couldn't help but smile as she remembered some of the contests they'd found themselves embroiled in. Their game of one-upsmanship had started in the first grade, when they worked to see who would be ranked higher on the honor roll at the end of each term. In middle school, they had competed to represent their class on the student council. By the time they reached high school, they were in an all-out race to see which one of them would be at the top of their graduating class. That particular competition had turned out to be a draw, and they ended up sharing the honor of being co-valedictorians.

Through it all, they had goaded, teased and thrown out challenges, and although their rivalry had never become a cutthroat battle, they hadn't been friends, either. That was why, earlier in the coat room when Brad had shown such genuine concern and compassion, he had thrown her off guard. Maybe that was the reason she had felt compelled to tell him about her infertility.

She took a deep breath. Her inability to bear a child wasn't something she discussed freely, and she couldn't believe that she had opened up to him about it. She hadn't even been able to bring herself to tell some of her close friends. Why had she shared one of her most painful secrets with him?

As she pondered her uncharacteristic behavior, Sunnie began to squirm within the confines of the baby carrier, and Abby knew she was about to wake up. If the infant's whimpering was any indication, she was working up a lusty cry. Before they disrupted the rest of Brad's speech, Abby grabbed the diaper bag and her purse, then picked up the baby from the carrier and walked to the double doors at the back of the room.

They hadn't been out in the main hall more than a few minutes when Brad—baby carrier in hand—and the other men running for the board joined them. "After the vote tomorrow, all we have to do is wait until the Christmas Ball to see who wins," he said, setting the carrier on the floor beside them.

"We're done for the day?" she asked, placing a pacifier to Sunnie's eager lips.

Brad nodded. "It's a good thing, too. I think I need to take this little lady home and give her a bottle before we both crash for the afternoon."

"Have you considered hiring a nanny?" Abby asked, patting the baby's back as she swayed from side to side in an effort to keep Sunnie calm.

"I don't intend to hire anyone to take care of Sunnie," he said, stubbornly shaking his head. "I took on the responsibility of raising her and that's what I fully intend to do. I'm not handing her care over to someone else, other than an occasional night out or a business meeting."

When he didn't elaborate, she felt compelled to ask, "How on earth are you going to manage taking care of her for the next couple of weeks without your housekeeper being around to advise you?" She hoped he was better at feeding a baby than he was at changing diapers.

Abby watched him run his hand through his thick, dark brown hair. She could tell he was a bit uneasy about being solely responsible for Sunnie's care. "I'll do my best, and if I run into something I can't handle,

I'll call my best friend Zeke Travers' wife, Sheila, or my sister, Sadie, for advice," he said decisively. "Sheila's a nurse and took care of Sunnie until I got custody. I'm sure if needed, one of them would be willing to come over and show me what to do." He smiled. "By the way, thank you for watching her while I finished my speech. I really appreciate it."

"I didn't mind at all." Setting the diaper bag on the floor, Abby knelt to place Sunnie in the carrier, then secured the straps and tucked a blanket in around her. "My ranch isn't far from your house. If you can't get hold of Sheila or Sadie, you can always give me a call and I'll try to answer whatever questions you might have."

"I'll keep that in mind," he said seriously.

When she stood up, they stared at each other for several long moments as they both realized the other candidates had left and they were alone.

He suddenly gave her a lopsided grin. "Have you looked up?"

"No," she answered slowly. "Should I?"

He pointed to something hanging from one of the heavy beams on the ceiling. "You're standing under the mistletoe."

"I hadn't…" her breath caught when he stepped forward and put his arms around her waist "…noticed." Surely he wasn't going to kiss her?

"I have to," he said, as if reading her thoughts. "It's a tradition."

Before she had the chance to remind him that they were opponents and that she wasn't interested in observing that particular custom with him or anyone else, his mouth settled over hers in a kiss so gentle it left her speechless. Firm and warm, his lips caressed hers with a mastery that confirmed all the rumors she had heard about him being a ladies' man. No man kissed that way without having one of two things—either a natural sense of what pleased a woman or a wealth of experience. Abby suspected that Bradford Price had an abundance of both.

Feeling as if her legs were about to fold beneath her, she reached up to put her hands on his wide shoulders. The solid strength she felt beneath the fabric of his black Armani jacket sent her heart racing and did nothing to help steady her wobbly knees. But when he wrapped his arms around her and pulled her more fully against him, her legs failed her completely and she sagged against him.

Thankfully Sunnie chose that moment to spit out her pacifier and wail at the top of her little lungs, effectively bringing Abby out of the spell Brad had put her under. Leaning back, she quickly looked around to see if anyone had been watching them. She was relieved to find that the hall was empty.

"I...need to...get my coat," she said, feeling as if the oxygen had been sucked from the room. "Sheila and I have...some shopping to do for the party...at the women's shelter."

"Yeah, I should get Sunnie home for a bottle and a nap." To her extreme displeasure, Brad didn't act as if he had been affected one darned bit by the kiss.

He stuck his hand out and without thinking, Abby reached out to shake it. The moment their palms touched, a warm tingling sensation streaked up her arm. She quickly drew back.

"May the best man—"

"Or woman," she automatically corrected him.

Shaking his head, he gave her that knowing grin of his—the one that never failed to make her want to bop him. "I suppose it won't hurt for you to hang on to that little dream until it's announced that I've won."

"Oh, don't worry, Price. I most certainly will," she said, with renewed determination. "I can't wait to see the look on your face when I win."

"We'll see about that, Langley." He picked up the baby carrier and diaper bag, then turned toward the exit. "If I were you I wouldn't start polishing your gavel just yet."

"I could say the same thing about you and your presidential gavel," she shot back.

His deep laughter as he walked down the hall and out of sight sent a wave of anger coursing through her. What on earth had gotten into her? Why had she let him kiss her? And why was she standing there like a complete ninny, watching him leave?

Unable to understand her atypical behavior, Abby started toward the coatroom. She wished she had the answers to why she'd acted so out of character, but at the moment nothing came to mind—other than she might have temporarily lost her mind.

Shaking her head, she pulled on her coat and walked to her car. She wasn't certain who she was more angry with, him for being so blasted arrogant or herself for letting him get away with it.

But one thing was crystal clear. Nothing like that

was going to happen again. Aside from the fact that she wasn't interested in being kissed by any man, she was far more comfortable dealing with Bradford Price her lifelong opponent than she would ever be with Brad Price—arguably the best kisser in southwest Texas.

Two

"Zeke, is Sheila at home?" Brad asked, as soon as his best friend answered the phone.

"Hey man, how are things going?" Zeke Travers asked cheerfully.

Brad tried to rub away the tension building at the back of his neck. "At the moment, not good."

"I can tell." Zeke laughed. "It sounds like Sunnie is throwing one grand and glorious fit. Where's Juanita?"

"Out of town and—"

"Uh-oh, you're on your own with the baby," Zeke finished for him.

"Yeah and she won't stop crying," Brad said, wondering how something as small as a baby could make so much noise. He was pretty sure her wailing had the dogs barking in downtown Royal. "I was hoping Sheila might have an idea of what could be wrong with her."

"Sorry, man. Sheila went with Abby Langley to do some shopping for the Christmas party they're throwing next week for the kids at the women's shelter over in Somerset." His friend paused. "Do you think Sunnie might be hungry? When Sheila took care of her, I noticed that Sunnie was pretty short on patience when she wanted a bottle."

"It hasn't been that long since I fed her, and everything was fine up until about ten minutes ago," Brad said miserably. "That's when she started crying, and she won't stop."

"Maybe she needs her diaper changed," Zeke suggested, sounding as mystified as Brad felt.

"I just put a new one on her." Brad walked over to the baby swing, where his niece sat screaming at the top of her lungs. "I've tried rocking her, holding her to my shoulder and walking the floor with her. Nothing seems to help. She normally likes her swing, but that isn't cutting it with her this evening, either."

"Man, I don't know what to tell you." Zeke paused. "Hang on a minute. Abby's car just pulled into the driveway. Let me fill Sheila in on what's going on and then have her call you back."

"Thanks, Zeke. I owe you one," Brad said, ending the call. He tossed the phone on the couch and picked up Sunnie to pace the floor with her again.

He hated having to bother Zeke and Sheila. They were newlyweds, and he was pretty sure they had more pleasurable things to do in the evenings than give him advice on how to care for a baby. But he was at his wit's end and man enough to admit that he needed help.

"It's okay, baby girl," he crooned as he patted her

back and walked from one room to another. "We'll get through this."

If anything Sunnie's screaming got louder and made him feel like a complete failure for the first time in his life. He had thought he was doing the right thing when he made the decision to adopt his late brother Michael's daughter. But if today was any indication of his parenting skills, he might have been wrong. Although he had gotten the hang of diapering and feeding Sunnie, it appeared he was a complete washout at knowing what was wrong and how to calm her.

What was taking Zeke and Sheila so long to return his call? he wondered, checking his watch. It had been a good ten minutes since Zeke assured him that Sheila would call him back.

With Sunnie wailing in his ear like a banshee gone berserk, it took a moment for Brad to realize that someone was ringing the doorbell. "Thank God," he muttered, as he rushed over to open the door. He fully expected to see Zeke and Sheila Travers standing on the other side. "I really appreciate—"

Instead of Sheila, Abigail Langley stood on the front porch with her hand raised to ring the doorbell again. Great. The last thing he needed was her witnessing yet another of his inadequacies in child care.

"I don't want to be here any more than you want me here," she said, as she hurried into the foyer. "But Sheila became ill while we were out shopping and asked me to stop by to check on you and Sunnie."

Apparently he hadn't been very good at hiding his displeasure at seeing her again. But Abby's help was better than no help at all, he quickly decided when the baby's screaming reached a crescendo. Explaining everything he'd tried to get Sunnie to stop crying, Brad shook his head. "Nothing works. She'll start to wind down and look like she's going to nod off, then she'll open her eyes and start screaming again. If she keeps this up much longer, I'm afraid she'll hurt herself."

Quickly removing her coat, Abby handed it and her purse to him as she reached to take the baby. "It's all right, angel. Help has arrived. Where's her pacifier?"

He handed Abby the one he had been trying to get Sunnie to take. "I don't think it will do any good. She keeps spitting it out."

As soon as Abby placed the pacifier in the baby's mouth and cradled her close, Sunnie's crying began to lessen. "Do you have a rocking chair?" Abby asked.

All she had to do was walk in the door and take the baby from him and Sunnie reduced the racket she was making by a good ten decibels. "What the hell does she have that I don't?" he muttered under his breath, as he laid Abby's coat and purse on a bench in the hall, then led the way to the family room.

Motioning toward the new rocking chair he'd bought the day before bringing Sunnie home from Sheila and Zeke's, Brad stuffed his hands into the front pockets of his jeans and watched as Abby seated herself and began to gently rock the baby. In no time at all Sunnie's cries had settled to occasional whimpers and he could tell she was about to go to sleep.

"When I tried rocking her, she just screamed louder," he said, unable to keep from feeling a bit resentful. The immediate change in the baby when Abby took her made him feel completely inept, and it annoyed him beyond words that she had been witness to it.

"I think the problem is that you're nervous about taking care of her without help." Abby shifted Sunnie from her shoulder to the crook of her arm. "She senses that."

"I don't get nervous," he said flatly. Frowning, he stubbornly shook his head. "I might feel a little apprehensive about being solely responsible for her care, but I'm not the nervous type."

Abby laughed softly. "Apprehension, nervousness, whatever you want to call it, I think she's picking up on it and she's letting you know the only way she can that it upsets her."

Feeling a little insulted, he glared at the woman calmly rocking his niece. "So you're saying it's my fault she wouldn't stop crying?"

Her indulgent smile as she shook her head had him clenching his teeth. "Not entirely. I think a big part of her problem is that she's fighting to stay awake."

Brad grunted. "I'd rather fight *for* sleep than against it."

She nodded. "Me, too. But with each day Sunnie is becoming more alert and aware of what's going on around her. I think she's probably afraid she'll miss something."

While Abby rocked the baby, Brad went into the kitchen to start a pot of coffee and see if there was some of Juanita's apple cake left. The least he could do was offer Abby cake and coffee for bringing the noise level down. When he returned to the family room, Sunnie was sound asleep.

"I don't think we should risk waking her when you pick her up," Abby said, her tone low.

"Good God, no." Just the thought of another crying marathon like the one that had just ended made him cringe.

Rising from the chair, she smiled. "If you'll tell me where the nursery is, I'll put her to bed for you."

He led the way up the stairs to the bedroom he'd turned into a nursery and couldn't help but notice how natural Abby looked with a baby in her arms. If any woman was meant to mother a child, it was Abigail Langley. It bothered him to think she wasn't going to give herself that chance.

He had come to fatherhood through adoption. She could reach motherhood that way, too. All she had to do was open herself to the possibility. But she apparently wasn't ready to consider her options and it wasn't his place to point out what they were.

While she put Sunnie to bed in the crib, he turned on the camera and picked up the video baby monitor to take with them. "Thank you for stopping by," he said once they'd left the nursery and were descending the stairs. "It seems like you've had to come to my rescue twice today."

She gave him a questioning look. "Since Sunnie is wearing a dry diaper, I assume you mastered that challenge?"

Nodding, he grinned. "It turned out to be a lot easier than getting her to bed for the night." When they reached the bottom of the stairs, he asked, "Would you like to stay for a cup of coffee and a piece of cake?"

"I…should go and let you enjoy the quiet," she said,

walking over to the bench where he had laid her coat and purse earlier. "If you have any more problems you can always call me."

Before she had a chance to pick up her things, he placed his hand to the small of her back and ushered Abby toward the family room. "To tell you the truth, I could use the company of another adult for a little while. As you've seen this evening, Sunnie isn't exactly a witty conversationalist just yet."

"No, but you have to admit, she gets her point across," Abby said, smiling.

"No kidding." He rubbed the side of his head. "I'm still experiencing some ringing in my left ear."

When they went into the family room, she sat down on the edge of the couch. "If you don't mind, I think I'll pass on the cake and coffee. If I drink caffeine now, I'll be up all night."

"Would you like something else?" He walked over to turn on the gas log in the fireplace. "I think there are some soft drinks in the fridge."

Abby shook her head. "I'm fine. Thank you."

"I'd offer you something stronger, but since I don't drink, I don't keep it around the house."

Brad's sister, Sadie, had told her that he never drank anything stronger than coffee or iced tea, due to the fact that their older brother, Michael, had been an alcoholic, as well as a drug addict. It had ultimately led to the man's death when, in a drug and alcohol induced haze, he'd crashed through a guardrail and driven over the side of a cliff.

"I'm not much of a drinker, either," she admitted.

"I might have an occasional glass of wine with dinner, but that's about it."

Brad sank into the big, overstuffed armchair flanking the couch. "Don't get me wrong. I have nothing against drinking in moderation. It's when a person doesn't know when to quit that it becomes a problem."

"Like it did for your brother?" she asked.

He nodded. "Mike had a rebellious streak a mile wide and would do anything he could think of to humiliate our dad. What better way to do it than to become the town drunk?"

She could tell Brad resented the fact that his brother had gone out of his way to humiliate the Price family. She could sympathize. In her senior year in high school she had suffered through her own family's scandal, and knowing they were the subject of intense gossip and speculation had been one of the worst times in her life.

"A lot of kids go through a reckless stage," she offered gently. "I'm sure Michael never meant for it to become the huge problem that it did for him."

"You're probably right. Unfortunately, Mike never seemed to be able to come out of that phase and it just got worse when Dad disowned him."

Two years older than she and Brad, all she could remember about Michael Price was that he had a reputation for partying hard and raising hell. "Was your dad disowning him the reason he left Royal?"

"Dad had reached the end of his rope," Brad said, nodding. "He ordered Mike out of the house and rather than stick around to see how Dad felt once he had cooled down, Mike took off. The first news we had of him was eight months ago when we were notified that he'd been killed."

"Michael's death must have broken your father's heart," she said, unable to imagine the degree of desperation Brad's father had to have reached to take such a drastic stand. To lose his son without making amends had to have been crushing.

"I'm sure it affected him more than he let show." Raising one dark eyebrow, Brad gave her a pointed look. "But don't get the idea that Robert Price would have handled it any other way. You know how he is about appearances. Sadie wouldn't have made the decision to move to Houston when she got pregnant with the twins if she hadn't been worried about our father's disapproval."

Abby had been in Seattle at the time, working at the web development company she and one of her college friends had started right after graduation. It wasn't until she sold her interest in the highly successful venture and moved back to Royal to marry Richard that she learned the story behind Sadie's move.

"I'm glad she decided to return to Royal," Abby said sincerely. "If she hadn't, she and Rick might not have run into each other."

Brad's sister had become pregnant after one night with Rick Pruitt, just before the dashing Marine had been deployed to the Middle East. Losing touch, it wasn't until some three years later that they were reunited when they ran into each other at the TCC clubhouse. Now they were happily married, raising their adorable two-year-old twin daughters and looking forward to a bright future together.

"Dad mellowed over the years and was pleased about her and the girls moving back, so it all worked out for the best." Brad glanced at the video monitor he still held. "Do you think Sunnie will be all right? She cried awfully hard there for a while."

"Babies do that." Abby couldn't help but be a bit amused. She had never seen Brad Price look more unsure of himself, and she found it oddly fascinating. "I think she'll be fine, Brad. Really."

"I hope that's the case," he said, placing the monitor on the end table beside his chair.

"This afternoon you mentioned that you don't intend to hire a nanny," she said, when he glanced at the monitor again as if needing to reassure himself that the baby was all right. "Having help might give you a bit more peace of mind about caring for her."

"I'm not entirely certain that handing Sunnie's care over to someone else would be in her best interest," he said, surprising her. His expression told her that he had given the matter a considerable amount of thought.

"You're going to try to do this on your own?" She hadn't meant to sound so incredulous, but men with the kind of fortune Bradford Price had amassed hired help to take care of their children, even if they were married.

"Yes, I am," he answered decisively. He sat forward, propping his forearms on his knees, and stared down at his hands as if trying to put his reasoning into words. "This isn't about me or my comfort. This is about Sunnie. In her short little life, she's been abandoned by her mother, used as a pawn in a blackmail scheme and passed from one stranger to another. She hasn't really had the chance to bond with anyone." His tone took on a hard edge. "She deserves a hell of a lot better than that."

Abby couldn't have agreed more. Sunnie had been the result of Michael Price's only night with an unscrupulous woman who, after giving birth, had tried using her infant daughter at the request of a dangerous drug lord to extort money from the Price family. They had sent blackmail notes to Brad, as well as a few other TCC members, telling each of them they were the father in an effort to get as much money as they could. He had correctly assumed they'd be too embarrassed to reveal to each other that they were being blackmailed. But when Brad and the other men who had received notes refused to pay, the career criminal had given up on his scheme and the mother abandoned the baby on the doorstep of the club with a note pinned to her blanket, declaring Brad was Sunnie's father. A DNA test proved that there was indeed a genetic link, but when Zeke Travers tracked down the baby's mother, she admitted that it was Michael Price and not Brad who had fathered Sunnie. Whether it was due to a sense of obligation to his late brother or the fact that Sunnie had captured his heart, Brad had taken responsibility for her and started the adoption process.

"I applaud your dedication," she said, choosing her words carefully. He was trying so hard to do the right thing for Sunnie, she certainly didn't want to discourage him. "But don't you think it would be wise to have a little help? At least until you become more accustomed to caring for her by yourself?"

"She's had so many people come and go in her life,

I want her to know that I'm not just another person taking care of her until the next one comes along." He shrugged. "I want her to know early on that I'm always going to be here for her. That's why I'm working from home for the next six months."

"You're serious," she said softly, in total awe of the lengths he was willing to go to for the baby girl.

"Very. My assistant is running the day to day operation at the firm and forwarding anything she can't handle through email and faxes. After Sunnie's first birthday, I'll see how things are going and make my decision whether to continue working from home or go back into the office."

Abby had gained a newfound respect for Brad when she heard he was taking on the responsibility of raising Sunnie as his own, but that admiration had just gone up a good ten notches. She knew a lot of men with his wealth and position in the business community who wouldn't even consider going to such lengths for their own children, let alone a niece or nephew they were adopting.

The contrast between Bradford Price, the playboy financial genius, and Brad Price, the dedicated new daddy, was disconcerting and Abby needed time to assimilate and understand the two sides of his personality. It had been much easier to view him as her life-long rival and fierce opponent in the race for the TCC presidency than it was to see him as the down-to-earth, caring man she had seen over the course of the day.

Needing to put distance between them, she made a show of checking her watch as she rose from the couch.

"I should go. I have to get up early tomorrow to help Summer Franklin with the charity drive."

"In other words, you're going to put those god-awful pink flamingos in some poor unsuspecting soul's front yard, so he'll have to donate money to the Helping Hands Women's Shelter to get rid of them," Brad said, getting up to walk her to the door.

"It's for a good cause," Abby defended.

"I'm not saying it isn't." Brad laughed. "But pink flamingos? Seriously, couldn't they come up with something a lot more attractive and a little less tasteless?"

She picked up her coat and purse as they passed the bench in the hall. "If they were attractive, people might not be as eager to get rid of them and donate less."

"I guess you have a point," he conceded. "But do me a favor."

"What's that?" she asked as he took her coat from her and held it while she put it on.

Placing his hands on her shoulders, he turned her to face him. "When you drive by my place, keep on going," he said, grinning. "I'll send in a donation just to keep from having to look at them." Before she realized what was happening, he wrapped his arms around her and pulled her close for a hug. "Thank you again for helping me out with Sunnie this morning and then again this evening. I really appreciate it, darlin'."

For some reason, the endearment most Texas men used freely when talking to a woman sent a shiver straight up her spine and the awareness she had experienced when Brad kissed her under the mistletoe came rushing back tenfold. When had the skinny kid she had always competed against developed so many muscles? And why did they feel so darned good pressed against her?

Hastily backing away from him, she walked to the door, hoping he hadn't noticed the fact that she had clung to him a little longer than was required for an embrace of appreciation. "If it gives you any measure of comfort, I can guarantee the pink flamingos won't be on your lawn tomorrow morning when you get up."

Grinning, he slipped his hands up to his thumbs into the front pockets of his jeans and rocked back on his heels. "That's good to know."

Stepping out onto the porch, she couldn't resist turning back for one parting shot. "But don't get too complacent, Price. Your day will come when you least expect it."

What was wrong with her? she wondered, as she walked to her car. Why after all these years was she suddenly noticing Brad's impressive muscles? How could it be that she felt more secure with his arms around her than she had in very long time? Had it been so long since she had been held by a man that even Bradford Price could make her feel breathless and cause her pulse to speed up?

"You've lost your mind, girlfriend," she muttered to herself as she steered her luxury SUV around the circular drive and out onto the street.

She wasn't looking to be held by any man, let alone a playboy like Bradford Price. With his piercing hazel eyes and dark good looks, he represented trouble with a great big capital T and she wanted no part of it.

Besides, after experiencing the pain of losing her

husband, she wasn't about to give her heart to another man and put herself in the position to go through something like that again. She was a survivor and it was only through working for various charities that she had kept herself going after the many disappointments of the past year. And although she did get lonely at times, community service would have to be enough for her. It was far less dangerous to her peace of mind than the almost irresistible combination of Bradford Price, with his rock-hard biceps and movie star good looks, and the most adorable baby girl Abby had ever seen.

"How much longer do you think we need to stay before it's socially acceptable to leave?" Brad asked Zeke, as he checked his watch.

If the informal cocktail party he was attending hadn't been in honor of the candidates for the various club offices, he would have declined the invitation. Instead, he had sipped on his club soda, engaged in the obligatory mingling with all of the other guests and counted the minutes until he could politely thank the election committee chairman, Travis Whelan, and his wife, Natalie, for hosting the party and leave.

"What's the rush?" Zeke asked, looking puzzled. "I thought you'd be glad to have an evening off from your child-care duties. After all, you've been on your own with Sunnie now for the past week."

Brad shrugged. "Sunnie isn't the easiest baby to get to sleep, and I'm pretty sure my sister will be ready to throw me to the coyotes by the time I get back."

"What happened to Bad Brad, the heartthrob of every sorority sister on the UT campus?" Zeke laughed.

"If you're not careful, you're going to ruin your reputation as a world-class player."

"The reports of my past conquests are greatly exaggerated," Brad said, grinning. "If you'll remember, I was the one sitting in our dorm room studying while you and Chris Richards were out on the town."

"Yeah, maybe once," Zeke shot back, his smile wide. "If you'll remember, Chris Richards and I were usually with you in those days and doing anything but studying."

As he and his best friend stood there reminiscing about their college days and their friend, Chris, another member of the TCC, Brad noticed Abby walk through the Whelans' front door. Wearing a pair of black slacks, a matching jacket and a pink silk blouse, she was utterly stunning. To his amazement, the sight of her robbed him of breath.

Maybe Zeke was right about his needing a night out, Brad decided, forcing himself not to stare. If the sight of his lifelong nemesis peaked his interest like this, then he was in definite need of some female companionship.

"Looks like Sheila's trying to get my attention," Zeke said, nodding toward his wife. "I'll bet she's not feeling well again and wants to go home."

"Has she seen a doctor?" Brad asked, concerned for the woman who would soon be Sunnie's godmother. He couldn't think of anyone else he'd rather have for the baby's godparents than the Traverses. Brad knew for certain that if anything happened to him, they would see that Sunnie was loved and cared for.

"Not yet," Zeke said, looking worried. "She has an

appointment tomorrow." He placed his champagne glass on a passing waiter's tray. "I'll see you the day after tomorrow at our meeting with the commissioner."

"Tell Sheila I hope she's feeling better soon," Brad said, as his friend started across the room toward his wife.

"I'm worried about Sheila," Abby said, walking over to him.

"So is Zeke, but I'm sure she'll be all right," Brad said, turning his attention to the woman beside him. "You look very nice this evening."

She gave him a suspicious look. "Really?"

Her question surprised him. "I wouldn't have said it if I hadn't meant it."

"In that case, thank you," she said, taking a sip of the drink she held.

"Why would you think I'm not sincere?" he asked, frowning.

"You have to ask?" Her laughter caused an unfamiliar warmth in his chest. "I'm not used to something like that from you, Price. Veiled insults and jokes at my expense—yes. Compliments—no."

Brad started to deny her claim, but with sudden clarity, he realized she was right. When she had joined the TCC, he had made comments and jokes about her that, looking back, he wasn't overly proud of. It was no wonder she didn't believe him when he made a favorable remark.

"I believe an apology is in order," he said, clearing his throat.

"You're out of your mind if you think I owe you an

apology, Price," she said incredulously. "Of all the arrogant—"

"Hush." Setting his drink on a nearby table, Brad took her by the elbow and led her out into the Whelans' enclosed courtyard before she drew too much attention to them. If he was going to have to eat crow, he didn't particularly want witnesses.

"What are you up to now, Price?" she demanded.

When they were safely out of earshot of anyone eavesdropping, he placed his hands on her shoulders to keep her from walking away. "If you'll stop jumping to conclusions and let me finish, I would like to tell you that my behavior the past several months has been out of line and uncalled for." He could tell by the widening of her vibrant blue eyes that it was the last thing she expected from him. "I'm sorry for that, Abby."

She shook her head. "I…um…don't know what to say."

"You could start by telling me you accept my apology." He shrugged. "But that's up to you."

"Y-yes…" She cleared her throat. "I accept."

"Good." He smiled. "Now that we have that out of the way, I want you to know that I meant what I said." He slowly slid his palms down her arms until he caught her hands in his, then stepped back and took in the sight of her. "You really do look incredible, Abby."

"Thank you," she said, her voice soft.

From the muted landscape lighting, he wasn't certain, but it looked as if she blushed. Fascinating. For reasons he didn't fully understand, Brad pulled her into his arms and held her close.

"What on earth do you think you're doing?" she asked, starting to pull away from him.

"I'm giving you a friendly hug to go along with my apology," he said, enjoying the feel of her lithe body pressed to his a little more than he anticipated. He felt a tiny shiver course through her and instinctively knew it had nothing to do with her being cold.

"When have we ever been friends?" she asked.

Releasing her, Brad stepped back. "Maybe it's about time to put this rivalry behind us and declare a truce."

She looked suspicious. "Why now after all these years?"

He shrugged. "Once I become the president of the TCC it would be nice to see unity restored to the club."

"Oh, really? *You're* going to win the presidency?" She laughed as she turned to walk back into the house. "I knew there had to be an underlying motive to your sudden generosity."

After watching her go inside, Brad stuffed his hands into his trouser pockets and stared up at the clear night sky. What the hell had gotten into him?

Lately, it seemed that he seized every opportunity to touch Abby, to hold her to him. It had started the other day at the clubhouse when she had helped him change Sunnie's diaper. He'd hugged her to offer his comfort when she told him about her inability to have children. But that didn't explain his kissing her under the mistletoe. And later that evening when she stopped by to help him get Sunnie to stop crying, he had told himself he hugged her out of gratitude. But the truth was, a simple thank-you would have sufficed.

Brad shook his head as he rejoined the party.

There was a simple explanation for his actions and it didn't take a genius to figure out what it was. He was a healthy male with a healthy appetite for the ladies. Since taking on the responsibility of his niece, he had curtailed his pursuit of female companionship, and it was only natural that he would gravitate toward Abby, since she was the only single female he'd had contact with in the past few weeks.

Satisfied that he had determined the reason for his uncharacteristic actions, Brad found the host and hostess, thanked them for the party and headed for the door. He would have to ask his sister to babysit again some evening in the near future in order for him to have a night out. Until then, he'd just have to make sure he steered clear of Abigail Langley.

Three

Brad smiled down at his niece as he placed the baby carrier in the shopping cart. "So far, so good, baby girl. You got a clean bill of health from the pediatrician and slept through the meeting with the commissioners from the football league. Now all we have to do is pick up more formula and diapers for you, a couple of frozen pizzas for me, as well as some stain remover for the clothing you've christened when you burp. Then we should be good to go home and crash."

After confirmation from the doctor today that Sunnie was perfectly healthy, Brad was doing his best to take whatever came along in stride and not worry so much about the things he couldn't change. It was a fact of life—babies cried. A lot. Sometimes there were tears, sometimes not. He had a strong suspicion that most times, Sunnie screamed at the top of her lungs just to keep him on his toes. But she had been an absolute angel this afternoon when he, Zeke and Chris Richards met with the minor-league football commissioner to work out the final details for the semipro team they were going to buy.

Just the thought of bringing the team to Royal made him smile. Like every other town in Texas, football was like a religion for the residents of Royal, and it had been a huge part of his life throughout high school and college. Playing quarterback, he, along with his two best friends, Chris and Zeke, had been a force to reckon with on the playing field, and he was happy to be partnering with them to bring the team to town. But they were going to wait until the night of the TCC Christmas Ball to make the official announcement. By that time, they hoped to have former pro player Mitch Hayward locked in as the team's general manager and Daniel Warren, the architect with the winning plans for the proposed new TCC building, working on designs for the new stadium they planned to have built.

As he pushed the cart down the grocery store aisle, he couldn't help but chuckle to himself. If someone had told him six months ago that he would trade going into the office for working from home in order to be available for diaper changes, or that he would be pushing a baby around the grocery store in a cart, he would have laughed his head off.

Looking up, Brad spotted Abby coming down the aisle toward him. Wearing boots, jeans, a pink T-shirt and a jeans jacket, her appearance was every bit the ranchwoman, and he couldn't stop himself from thinking about how good she looked.

He frowned. That was twice in the past few days that he'd found himself thinking of Abby as being attractive. Now he knew for certain he was in need of an evening out with a warm, willing female. As soon as he got home, he fully intend to call Sadie and arrange for her to babysit Sunnie one evening at her earliest convenience.

Satisfied with his plan of action, he couldn't help but smile.

"You seem to be quite pleased with yourself about something, Mr. Price." Abby tilted her head slightly. "Still anticipating that big win you're so sure of?"

"Of course." Feeling that he had regained his perspective, he nodded. "I'm as sure of winning the presidency as you are of beating me out of it."

"As a matter of fact, I'm going to do just that." She walked over to smile down at the baby. "How's the little angel?"

"Sunnie got a clean bill of health from the doctor this afternoon and didn't cry too much when he gave her an immunization shot." He grinned. "We're going to celebrate with a bottle for her and a frozen pizza for me, and veg out tonight in front of the TV."

"I assume the pediatrician told you there might be a reaction and what to watch for?" she asked, as she tickled Sunnie's chin.

The baby gave Abby a toothless grin and a gurgling laugh.

He glanced at his happy niece. "The doctor covered everything. Sunnie didn't like the shot much, but she's doing great. Rest assured, I'm getting the hang of taking care of her, and I don't anticipate that we'll have any more problems."

Abby raised her gaze to meet his. "I hope not."

Her doubtful expression rubbed him the wrong way. "We'll be just fine. I even figured out that getting her to go to sleep at night is a lot easier if she doesn't know that's what I'm doing."

To his immense irritation, Abby laughed out loud. "Oh, this should be good. Do tell what your secret is, Mr. Price."

"Why don't you stop by this evening to see for yourself?" he found himself asking. He could tell she didn't believe him, and it suddenly became a challenge to prove her wrong.

Some habits were hard to break, he decided, as he stared at the woman in front of him. For as long as he could remember, whenever Abby threw down a gauntlet he hadn't been able to resist picking it up—the same as she couldn't pass up answering his challenges.

She shook her head, and her long auburn ponytail swayed from side to side. "As much as I'd like to see this great feat of parenting you seem so proud of, I'm going to have to pass. I've been working around the ranch all day and I'm pretty tired."

"Afraid to see that I'm right and that I have it all worked out, are you?" he goaded.

Her vivid blue eyes narrowed. "Maybe I just don't want to witness your embarrassment when you fall flat on your face."

"I don't believe that for a minute," he said, shaking his head. "You'd like nothing better than to see me fail at something and we both know it."

"I do admit it's tempting," she said, glancing down at the baby. "But I—"

"Great. Do you like pepperoni, sausage or just plain cheese?"

She frowned. "I didn't say I would be—"

"It doesn't matter. I'll just pick up a variety of frozen pizzas, and you can choose when you get to my place." He quickly started pushing the cart toward the end of the aisle. "Sunnie and I will see you around six-thirty."

Before she had a chance to call out a refusal, he turned the corner and headed straight for the freezer section of the store. Abby might have gotten away with declining, had he not seen her resistance as a contest of wills.

Brad smiled down at Sunnie happily playing with her fingers. "I came out on top in this round, but you have to help me out with the next one. Abby doesn't believe I can get you to go to sleep without you screaming like a cat with its tail caught in the door. We're going to prove her wrong, aren't we?"

Sunnie's high-pitched squeal of laughter encouraged him.

"Great," he said, heading for the checkout counter. "Keep up your end of the bargain, and I'll buy you a new car when you turn sixteen."

After parking her SUV in the circular drive in front of Brad's house, Abby shook her head as she prepared to get out of the car. She had to have lost what little mind she had left or else she would be home curled up on the couch reading a book instead of walking up to knock on Brad's door.

She had spent the past couple of hours at war with herself. As much as she wanted to be around Sunnie, Abby wasn't at all comfortable with being around the baby's uncle. She had even gotten as far as picking up the phone to call and tell him that something had come up and she wouldn't be over after all.

But the lure of holding and playing with the beautiful baby girl had won out. Sunnie had remained happy and extraordinarily well-adjusted despite being handed from one person to another for the first few months of her life, and Abby was finding it impossible to pass up an opportunity to be with the precious little bundle of joy. Unfortunately, the baby came along with six feet two inches of pure trouble, and to her displeasure she was suddenly finding Brad to be the best-looking, most intriguing trouble she'd seen in a very long time.

Sadie had jokingly told her on more than one occasion that Brad had made it his mission in life to date every available woman in Royal, earning him the reputation of being a player. But it appeared that he had given up his playboy lifestyle in favor of caring for the tiny six-month-old little girl, and without the benefit of a nanny. Very few men she knew would even consider something like that, let alone actually do it. Brad seemed to be trying so hard to be a good parent to Sunnie, and Abby couldn't help but find that endearing and, much to her bewilderment, quite sexy. If that wasn't proof enough that she had lost what little sense she had left, she didn't know what was.

Promising herself that she would stay only a few minutes, then find an excuse to leave, Abby took a deep breath and knocked on the door. When Brad opened it a moment later, her breath caught and her heart skipped several beats. He held Sunnie in one arm and had a black T-shirt draped over the other arm.

"Y-you aren't wearing a shirt."

"Really? I hadn't noticed," he said, his voice filled with laughter.

She hadn't meant to blurt out the obvious, but she had never seen so many impressive ripples and ridges on a chest and abdomen in her entire life. Gulping, she couldn't seem to avert her eyes. Had he always had shoulders that wide and a waist that trim? She couldn't stop her gaze from following the narrow line of dark hair that ran from his navel down his flat lower belly to disappear beneath the waistband of his jeans. Jeans that rode low on narrow hips and emphasized his well-defined flank muscles.

Good Lord, the man had been hiding a fabulous body beneath those Armani suits all this time, and she hadn't had a clue. Her cheeks heated and she averted her gaze as she forced herself to walk past him and into the foyer.

"Would you mind holding Sunnie while I put on my shirt?" he asked, closing the door behind her. "She's been fussy since we got home and wants to be held all of the time."

Brad was apparently oblivious to her shocked reaction at the sight of his magnificent body, and Abby was just as glad that he hadn't noticed. She was having enough trouble coming to terms with the effect he was having on her, she didn't need to deal with him commenting on it.

Taking the baby from him, she watched as he pulled

on the black T-shirt. "I think babies are nauseated by the smell of clean shirts," he said, shaking his head as he tucked the tail of the garment into his jeans. "Every shirt I own has a stain on it."

"Don't you drape a burp cloth over your shoulder when you give her a bottle?" Abby asked, concentrating on the little girl in her arms. It was much safer to give Sunnie her undivided attention than it was to watch Brad.

Putting his hand to her back, he nodded as he guided her toward the family room. She did her best to ignore the warmth that radiated throughout her body from his touch.

"I try using one of those whenever I feed her," he said, chuckling. "But there are times when the cloth slips or she grabs it with her fist and it gets pulled out of the way. The result is me having to change shirts a lot."

"If it's any consolation, she should be coming out of the worst of it within another month or so," Abby assured him, continuing to stare down at the baby in her arms. It was far less dangerous than looking at Sunnie's uncle. "Normally, having to be burped tapers off around the age of six months for an infant—about the time she starts sitting by herself."

"You know a lot about babies." His smile caused her to catch her breath. How could she have gone all these years without realizing, until just recently, how good-looking he was?

"There for a while, I read everything I could about babies and all the stages of their development," she said, concentrating on how she was going to make a graceful but hasty exit. "That was—"

"When you and Richard first started trying to have a baby?" he asked, his tone gentle.

She hesitated a moment, then nodded. "Yes."

It was easier to let him think that the only time she had studied the stages of an infant's development was when she and her husband first started trying to get pregnant. Explaining the last time she had thought there would be a baby in her future was still too painful to share with anyone.

They fell silent until Sunnie laid her head on Abby's shoulder and she noticed the baby felt warmer than normal. "Uh-oh. Brad, do you have a thermometer?"

"There was one of those digital kind that you stick in the baby's ear in Sunnie's things when I brought her home from Sheila's," he said, nodding. "Why?"

Abby placed her cheek to Sunnie's. "I think she's running a little bit of a fever."

"Should I call the pediatrician?" he asked, a worried frown suddenly creasing his forehead.

She shook her head. "Not yet. Go get the thermometer. We need to check what her temperature is first."

"Be right back," he said, taking off down the hall at a jog. When he returned, he handed her the electronic device as he reached for the baby. "I'm not exactly sure how this works. Why don't I hold her while you take the reading?"

Gently placing the thermometer in Sunnie's ear, she pushed the button. The reading appeared on the digital screen almost instantly. "She is running a low-grade fever."

"How high is it?" he asked, clearly alarmed.

"It's only slightly elevated," she assured him. "Did the doctor tell you what kind of fever reducer to use in case she had a reaction to the shot he gave her this afternoon?"

Brad nodded as he placed the baby back in her arms. "He had me pick up some drops from the pharmacy. Do you think that could be what's happening?"

"I think that's probably it." She gave him a reassuring smile as she lowered herself and the baby into the rocking chair. "It's not at all uncommon for a baby to be fussy and run a bit of a temperature after a vaccination."

While Brad went to get the medication, she held Sunnie close and rubbed her back to soothe her. "It's all right, little one. You'll feel better soon." Abby had no sooner gotten the words out than she felt something wet against her shoulder. "Hmm, looks like I should have practiced what I preached about those burp cloths, doesn't it?"

"It says we can give this to her every four to six hours," Brad said, reading the directions on the small box he held as he walked back into the room.

"I can help you with the first dose," Abby said, when he walked over to stand beside the rocking chair. "But I have to leave after that."

"Why?" he asked, looking alarmed.

She pointed to the wet spot on her shoulder. "You might have been right about the smell of clean clothes nauseating babies."

"So she got you too, huh?" He chuckled as he filed the dropper with the recommended dosage of fever reducer and gave it to Sunnie. "There's no need for you to go. You can wear one of my shirts."

That sounded way more cozy than she was comfortable with. "Thank you, but—"

He squatted down in front of her and placing his hands on the arms of the rocking chair, effectively trapped her. "I hate to admit this, Abby, but since this is the first time Sunnie has been sick, I'd feel more comfortable if you stayed for a while." When he reached up to touch the baby's cheek, the backs of his fingers brushed Abby's breast. "At least until her fever is gone."

Abby could understand Brad's apprehension. He was just getting comfortable with caring for Sunnie, and it had to be intimidating now that he was faced with her first illness, even if it was a minor reaction to an immunization. But the feel of his hand against her sensitive skin even through her clothing sent an awareness coursing through her that set off alarm bells deep in her soul. She needed to make her excuses and leave. Now.

"I'm sure Sheila or Sadie would be more than willing to come over and help you with Sunnie," Abby said, intrigued by his uncertainty. It was a side of Brad she had never seen before, and she found it to be in direct contrast to the self-assured, independent man she had known all of her life and, to her complete disconcertion, oddly endearing.

He shook his head. "Zeke and Sheila have gone out of town for the weekend, and Sadie, Rick and the girls have gone over to Somerset for the annual Christmas Lights Festival."

Abby might have been able to refuse him, but she

made the mistake of looking into his piercing hazel eyes. She had never seen him look more worried and as unwise as it was, she rationalized that he didn't have anyone else to help him. "Well, maybe for just a little while."

His relief was evident in the easing of the tension lines bracketing his mouth. "I'll get you one of my shirts to change into," he said, rising to his feet.

It crossed her mind to tell him not to bother. Wearing someone's shirt seemed a little too intimate for two people who had spent the majority of their lives in competition with each other. But the spot on her blouse was rather large, and the damp silk against her skin was pretty uncomfortable.

"Here you go," he said, returning to the family room to hand her a soft cotton T-shirt. "The guest bathroom is just off the hall to your right." He reached for the baby. "Besides giving her the drops for her fever, is there anything else we should do?"

Abby tried to think of what else she had read about infants running temperatures. "I don't think giving her water or formula would be a good idea. Do you have a bottle of liquid electrolyte replacement? That would be the best to give to her while she has a fever."

"If I don't, I'll go into town and get some."

"Where did you put all of the things Sheila sent over?" She started down the hall. "As soon as I change, I'll check to see if you have some."

"I put everything in the pantry," he answered.

Quickly finding the guest powder room, Abby eyed the shirt Brad had given her to put on as she unbuttoned her blouse. Thankfully it was heather gray and a little thicker than the average T-shirt. At least her bra wouldn't show through as much as it would have if the shirt had been white.

As she pulled it over her head, it was as if the man waiting for her just down the hall surrounded her. She closed her eyes as she savored his clean, masculine scent. There was only one word to describe the smell and that was…sexy.

Her eyes snapped open and she shook her head at her own foolishness. Brad might smell good—maybe even downright delicious—but she couldn't let herself be interested in anyone, especially the man who had been a thorn in her side all of her life.

Besides, caring for anyone was just too dangerous to her peace of mind. She and her mother had both suffered broken hearts when Abby's father had abandoned them for a life with his young secretary. Then, just when she had decided to take a chance on love, she had been devastated when her husband, Richard, suffered the aneurysm that took his life a little over a year ago. But the most recent heartbreak had been just a few months ago, when the mother of the baby she was supposed to adopt changed her mind. Abby had vowed afterward that there wouldn't be another chance of her losing someone she loved.

Taking a deep breath, she squared her shoulders and reached for the doorknob. She would help Brad with his adorable baby niece, then remove herself from the situation as soon as possible.

"I think she's finally gone to sleep," Brad said, careful to keep his voice low. He and Abby had taken turns all evening, rocking and walking the floor with Sunnie. "Do we dare try to take her temperature again?"

Nodding, she hid a yawn behind one delicate hand. "It was almost normal the last time we took it, and I'd really like to know that the fever has run its course before I leave."

As he picked up the thermometer and walked over to the rocking chair where she sat holding Sunnie, he glanced down at Abby. When they had run into each other in the grocery store that afternoon, she mentioned working all day around her ranch and she had just spent the entire evening helping him take care of a sick infant. She had to be dead on her feet, and he didn't think it was a good idea for her to drive home as tired as she was. But knowing Abby, if he insisted that she stay the rest of the night, she would leave just to spite him.

When he checked the digital screen on the thermometer, the numbers were normal. Breathing a sigh of relief he started to tell Abby, but her eyes were heavy lidded, and he could tell she was having to fight to stay awake.

"What's the verdict?" she asked, sounding as tired as she looked.

"Still slightly elevated," he lied. He hated not telling the truth, but he wasn't willing to take the risk of her falling asleep behind the steering wheel and having a car accident on the drive back to her ranch. He couldn't have that on his conscience. "Why don't you let me take Sunnie, while you stretch out on the couch and rest? If you go to sleep, I'll wake you when it's your turn to be up with her."

Before she had a chance to protest, he took Sunnie from her and, cradling the baby in one arm, helped Abby to her feet and guided her to the couch. "I think Sunnie is going to be fine," she said, sounding exhausted. "I'll just go on home and if you have any further problems, you can always call me."

"You know so much more about taking care of babies than I do. I'd really feel more at ease if you stay," he said, thinking quickly.

He purposely didn't tell her that at the moment it was her welfare and not Sunnie's that concerned him. Even if he told her, she probably wouldn't believe it.

Abby hesitated. Then just when he thought she was going to refuse, she sat down on the couch and removed her shoes. "I'll just lean my head back against the cushion and rest my eyes. Let me know when you need me to take over."

"Will do," he said, smiling.

Abby hadn't much more than rested her head against the back of the couch, and he could tell by her even breathing that she had already fallen asleep. He glanced down at the sleeping baby girl in his arms and hoped that she wouldn't wake up when he put her in the portable crib he had set up earlier. Once he had Sunnie down and he was assured she was resting peacefully, he turned his attention to the woman across the room. He wasn't about to wake her, but if he didn't try to get her into a more comfortable position, her back and neck were going to be stiff as hell by morning.

Sitting on the end of the couch, Brad reached to take Abby into his arms and pull her over against his shoulder. For a moment, he thought he'd awakened her, but instead of sitting up and demanding to know what he was doing, she placed her hand on his chest and snuggled closer. Her soft breath on the side of his neck immediately sent a wave of awareness to every cell in his body and had him cursing himself as a fool for making the noble gesture.

He closed his eyes and tried to think about something—anything—that would get his mind off of the woman lying against him. Starting out with his stats as quarterback in high school and college, by the time he had run through every football play he had called in every game, he gave up.

All he could think about was how good her body felt cuddled against his and how much he had enjoyed her unexpected reaction to seeing him with his shirt off when she first arrived for the evening. Abby might have thought she hid it, but her eyes were so expressive there was no way he could have missed her perusal of his body. He hadn't planned to answer the door bare chested, but he sure wasn't sorry it worked out that way.

His heart stalled, then pounded against his ribs. Why was it that lately every time he was around Abby, his libido went on full alert and he started thinking of her as an attractive, desirable woman?

For years, Abigail Langley was his nemesis and he was quite comfortable with that. Oh, there had been a time in high school that he had been attracted to her—even contemplated asking her to one of the homecoming dances. But Abby had eyes only for Richard Langley, and Brad had quickly reverted back to thinking of her as his rival and moved on to pursuing the girls on the cheerleading squad—all eight of them.

Back then, he had been looking at her with the innocent eyes of a youthful crush and would have been happy with a good-luck kiss and hug behind the bleachers before a game. But now? He was a man with a man's needs. A man who hadn't been with a woman in a while, and what he was thinking—feeling—at the moment, was anything but innocent.

When her hand slipped from his chest to his stomach, he gritted his teeth and shifted to relieve the rapidly building pressure against his fly. He had only thought to make her more comfortable, but in doing so he had succeeded in causing himself a great deal of discomfort.

Brad took a deep breath and concentrated on getting his body to relax. He wasn't sure why, but it appeared that he had come full circle. He was once again looking at Abby as more than his competitor. The only difference between now and their high school days was that this time she was looking back.

Four

When Abby opened her eyes, any traces of sleep that might have been lingering were instantly chased away as several things became apparent all at once. It was morning, she wasn't at home in her bed and her head was pillowed on…Brad's thigh.

Turning her head, she looked up to find him smiling down at her. "Good morning, Ms. Langley. Did you sleep well?"

"I…uh, yes." Good lord, how had she ended up with her head on his lap? The last thing she remembered was agreeing to stretch out for a few minutes until it was her turn to take care of the baby again.

She sat up and pushed her hair back away from her face. "How is Sunnie? Is her temperature down?"

He nodded. "She's doing just fine. Her fever broke around midnight."

"I wanted to go home." She wasn't the least bit happy with the situation. "Why didn't you wake me?"

He reached out to brush a wayward strand of her unruly hair from her cheek, sending a shiver of awareness straight up her spine. "The reason I let you sleep was because you were dead tired and I wasn't about to let you drive home and run the risk of you falling asleep at the wheel."

"You weren't about to *let me drive* home?" She could appreciate his concern, but the implication that she was incapable of making the decision herself was, in her estimation, out of line. "Let me tell you something, Mr. Price. I don't need your approval or permission to—"

Before she could finish telling him what she thought of his high-handedness, he pulled her into his arms. When his mouth came down on hers, Abby's first thought was to free herself, then bop him a good one. But the feel of his firm lips on hers, of his arms closing around her to pull her to his wide, solid chest, sent a shock wave straight through her, and she couldn't seem to work up even a token protest.

When he deepened the kiss and explored her with a thoroughness that stole her breath, her heart beat double time and a delightfully lazy warmth began to spread through every cell in her body. If she'd thought the kiss he gave her under the mistletoe at the TCC clubhouse had been moving, it had only been a glimpse of the skill and mastery Brad was showing her now.

Lightly stroking her tongue with his, he coaxed and teased until she felt herself responding in kind. With her hands trapped between them, she felt the steady beating of his heart beneath his padded pectoral muscles and she couldn't resist testing the strength of his chest with her palms. Bringing her arms up to encircle his shoulders, she gave in to the temptation of exploring the width and corded sinew there as well.

He brought his hand up to cup her breast, sending tingles of excitement racing up her spine and a jolt of longing through every part of her. It had been over a year since Abby had experienced the stirrings of passion and desire. The fact that she felt them in Brad Price's arms was not only unbelievable, it scared her as little else could. Because in Brad's arm, the feelings were stronger than she would have thought possible with any man.

Gathering the shreds of what was left of her good sense, she tried to put space between them, but he continued to hold her in a loose embrace. "Th-that shouldn't...have happened," she said, struggling to catch her breath.

"Probably not." His hazel eyes seemed to see right through her as they stared at each other. "But I'll be damned if I'm sorry it did, darlin'."

What was he trying to do to her and why? Was this some kind of ploy to get her to drop out of the race for the TCC presidency before the ballots were counted, giving him the office by default?

"What are you up to, Brad?" She hadn't meant to sound quite so accusatory, but she refused to apologize for asking the uppermost question running through her mind.

Before he could reply, the distinct sound of someone clearing their throat drew both of their attention. "I knocked, but when there was no answer, I used the key you gave me. I just stopped by to see how you're faring alone with the baby," Sadie said, grinning like a Cheshire cat. She was standing in the doorway leading to the kitchen and couldn't have looked more smug. "But I see that everything is under control here." She took a step backward. "Feel free to continue what you were doing. I let myself in. I can see my way out."

"No, don't go," Abby said, glaring at an unrepentant Brad. It appeared that he was going to just sit there grinning like his sister, leaving it up to her to make excuses. "I was just getting ready to leave myself."

"Go ahead and continue…talking," Sadie said, taking another step backward. "I really need to get over to the women's center to help sort through the toys that have been donated for the children's party."

"I was supposed to help with that," Abby said, wondering where her shoes were.

"I'll tell everyone that something came up and you won't be able to make it today," Sadie said, as she turned to leave.

"Well, she's right about one thing." Abby knew from his wicked grin what Brad was thinking. "Something did—"

"Don't even think about saying it," she warned.

Abby's cheeks felt as if they were suddenly on fire and she couldn't think of a solitary thing to say that wouldn't make things worse. She closed her eyes and tried to will away the entire situation. Unfortunately, when she opened them again, she was still in Brad's house, on his couch with his arms loosely wrapped around her.

"I've got to get out of here," she muttered, breaking free of his embrace to look for her shoes.

When she rose to her feet, he got up to stand beside her. "Thank you for spending the night with me."

"I was here because Sunnie needed me."

His knowing grin told her that he wasn't going to let it go. "You woke up with your head in my lap this morning. I think that means you were here with me all night. And if you want to get technical, we were both asleep—together."

"Don't even go down that road, Price." She shook her head. "I did not sleep with you."

"Well, there's sleeping and then there's *sleeping*," he said, laughing.

She refused to play his silly little word game as she looked around for the blouse he had laundered for her earlier. "Where's my shirt?"

"It isn't dry yet." His grin widened. "Since it was silk, I didn't think putting it in the dryer would be a good idea. You'll have to come back this evening to pick it up."

Turning to glare at him, she shook her head. "You can keep it."

"I appreciate the offer, but it's not my color." His rich laughter sent a tingle skipping over every nerve in her body. "Besides, you look a lot better in my shirt than I would in yours."

If she could have found her handbag, she would have bopped him for sure. "Where are my purse and shoes?"

"I hung your coat and purse in the guest closet just off the foyer," he said, bending down to reach for something under the coffee table. "Your shoes are right here."

"Thank you," she said, taking the cross-trainers from him. Seating herself on the armchair farthest from him, she put them on and stood up. "I'll have my ranch foreman drop your shirt off when he goes into Royal for supplies later on this week."

Brad shook his head. "No need. I'll get it from you the next time I see you."

Deciding it would be better to leave than to stand there and debate the point with quite possibly the most infuriating man she had ever met, Abby walked down the hall to the foyer closet. Not at all surprised that he followed, she put on her coat, then turned to face him.

"I think it would be a good idea for you to make sure Sheila or Sadie is around the next time there's a problem with the baby," she said, regretfully.

Not seeing Sunnie or being able to hold the baby would be difficult, but it was a matter of self-preservation. The more she was around the sweet baby girl and her exasperating uncle, the more it reminded Abby of what she wanted most in the world, but couldn't have—a family of her own.

Instead of arguing, as she thought he would, Brad simply stared at her for several long moments before he finally shrugged. "We'll see."

It wasn't the answer she expected, but it was apparently the best she was going to get from him. At least for now. "I'll see you at the Christmas Ball," she said, walking across the foyer to open the door.

"Oh, I'm sure we'll see each other before then." The

sound of the baby awaking drew their attention. "That's my call," he said, smiling. "See you later."

After watching him turn to go attend to the baby, Abby quietly closed the door behind her and walked to her SUV. Why did she feel as if she was taking the "morning after" walk of shame?

Nothing had happened last night and other than that steamy kiss this morning it wasn't going to. Ever.

She had stayed the night, to help Sunnie get through the reaction to her immunization shot. Period. The fact that Brad had taken it upon himself not to awaken her for the drive home wasn't her fault, and she refused to take the blame for it. He was also responsible for the kiss this morning. She certainly hadn't initiated it, and the fact that she hadn't discouraged it was immaterial. He'd simply taken her by surprise, and she had ended it as soon as she had been able to gather her wits about her.

Satisfied that she had things back in perspective, she got into the SUV and started the engine. As she steered it down the long drive toward the main road, she went over her plans for the day. She intended to take a shower, call Sadie for an impromptu lunch after they finished sorting toys at the women's center and do a little damage control.

Once Sadie heard the explanation for why she had seen them kissing, Abby was certain her best friend would understand. After all, Sadie was Brad's sister and knew how incorrigible the man could be.

Abby sighed heavily as she turned the Escalade onto the private road leading up to the big sprawling ranch house she had shared with Richard. Maybe if she kept telling herself how easily her actions could be explained and how innocent she had been in the whole matter, she might even start to believe it herself.

Seated in a booth at the Royal Diner, Abby anxiously awaited the right moment in her conversation with Sadie. She had gone over what she wanted to say at least a dozen times before she settled on just the right words to explain her atypical behavior with Brad. She didn't have long to wait.

"Okay, I assume you wanted to have lunch for the post-mortem of that kiss," Sadie said, smiling.

Abby was so preoccupied that she'd failed to notice Sadie had stopped talking about the cultural center she wanted to build. "There's a simple explanation for what you saw," Abby said, unable to keep the defensiveness from her tone.

Sadie grinned. "There always is."

"It was your brother's fault," Abby heard herself saying.

Her talk with Brad's sister wasn't going the way Abby had planned. She was supposed to remain calm and collected, not feel as if she had been caught making out with the high school football captain.

The woman across the chipped Formica table nodded. "Oh, I don't doubt Brad was the instigator. But what I want to know is why you let him get away with it?"

"We were arguing and—"

"He kissed you to shut you up," Sadie finished for her. Shaking her head, she laughed. "But that doesn't explain your reaction."

Before Abby could respond, a young waitress walked over to take their order. "What can I get for you ladies? The cook just made a new pot of his world famous chili, if you'd care to try that," she suggested, snapping the gum she was chewing.

"Hi, Suzy. Chili would be fine," both women said in unison.

"Bring us a couple of sweet teas with lemon, too," Sadie added.

Nodding, Suzy smiled. "Be right back with your order."

As if by unspoken agreement, Abby and Sadie both waited for their lunch to be served before they got back to the topic of the kiss.

"So tell me why you didn't stop my charming brother from giving you one of the steamiest kisses I've ever seen," Sadie said, picking up a cracker to dip into her bowl. "And why you were kissing him right back."

"He took me by surprise," Abby said, hoping her explanation didn't sound as lame to Sadie as it did to her.

"Abigail Langley, this is me you're talking to." Sadie shook her head. "I know you as well as anyone, and if you hadn't wanted Brad's kiss, you would have stopped it before it ever got started."

Abby opened her mouth to refute what her friend said, but quickly snapped it shut. Sadie was right. She could have called a halt to the embrace way before she had. Why hadn't she?

To her relief Sadie was on a roll and saved her from having to make a comment. "What were you doing at his house to begin with? You and Brad have been sworn enemies since grade school. I was under the impression that hadn't changed, and especially with the two of you running for TCC president."

"I…that is…" She stopped to take a deep breath. "It's complicated."

With her spoon halfway to her mouth, Sadie stopped, then placed it back into the bowl. "You wanted to see Sunnie again, didn't you?" she asked gently.

Seizing on the explanation provided by her friend, Abby nodded. They both knew how much Abby had wanted a child and how concerned she had been for the baby girl from the moment Sunnie had been left on the TCC's doorstep. But seeing the baby meant spending time with her infuriating, sexy-as-sin uncle. How could she put into words her conflicted feelings for the man when she didn't fully understand them herself? How could she possibly explain that as angry as he made her, she felt more alive when she was around him than she had in a very long time?

"Am I that transparent?" she asked, more comfortable with Sadie's explanation than she was her own.

"I understand." Placing her hand over Abby's, Sadie gave it a gentle squeeze. "I know how much it must hurt to want a baby and not be able to have one. But when you're ready, there are alternatives, Abby. You could always adopt a child."

Knowing that Sadie was only trying to help, Abby nodded. Sadie had no way of knowing that Abby's dream of becoming a mother had ended on that front as well.

She took a deep breath. "Maybe one day I'll consider it."

They were silent for a time before Sadie asked, "So how are you planning on getting even with my brother for taking advantage of the situation?"

"Hopefully, I'll win the TCC office and prove to him once and for all that I'm quite serious about my membership in the club." Abby took a sip of her iced tea. "I might have been accepted into the fold because of an obscure bylaw, but that doesn't mean that I don't intend to get involved."

"Well, you know I'm pulling for you," Sadie said, sitting back against the red vinyl upholstery. "Brad is so set in his ways, it's past time that someone turned his carefully crafted world upside down."

Abby laughed. "I think taking responsibility for Sunnie has been a good start. When Juanita left to go to Dallas the other day, he didn't even know how to fasten a disposable diaper."

Sadie nodded. "That's true. He loves my twins and he's a fantastic uncle. But I lived in Houston when the girls were babies. He wasn't around to help or witness the sleepless nights and hectic pace I had to keep in order to care for them."

"I'd say he's learning," Abby said, grinning. Deciding it was time to change the subject, she asked, "Have you had any more luck with finding a building for the Family Cultural Center?"

"I'm hoping the TCC will decide to build a new clubhouse and donate the current building to my foundation," Sadie said, looking hopeful. "Do you have any idea how that vote is going to go? With the economy the way it is, there's a real need for a place families in crisis can turn to for help."

Shaking her head, Abby picked up the check that Suzy had brought to them. "The last I heard, the membership was split right down the middle. The old guard wants to stick with tradition and stay in the original clubhouse and the new members want to build the design Daniel Warren presented."

As they slid from the booth and walked to the cash register at the end of the lunch counter, Sadie looked at the clock on the wall above the door. "I have to run." She gave Abby a hug. "Let me know if you hear anything about it one way or the other. I'd like to get started as soon as possible."

"I will," Abby said, as she paid the bill.

When she walked out of the diner and headed for her car, a note on the windshield drew her attention, and an immediate sense of apprehension surrounded her. It was all too reminiscent of the notes Brad and other members of the TCC had received in months past, claiming Sunnie was their child.

She took a deep breath and reached for the piece of paper. There wasn't any reason to be concerned. Zeke Travers had solved the mystery of the blackmail notes when he investigated who Sunnie's father was. The career criminal who had written them would be spending the rest of his life in jail for a variety of crimes.

Opening the folded paper, her eyes widened. It was from Brad, telling her that he and Sunnie would be visiting her ranch that evening. Abby looked around to see if he was anywhere in sight. The parking lot and street in front of the diner were deserted.

Hadn't she made it clear that she wanted him to look to others for help when he had problems with the baby?

Fit to be tied, she stuffed the note in her coat pocket and got into her SUV for the drive back to her ranch. It appeared Brad Price was deliberately tormenting her, and she had every intention of putting a stop to it.

If he showed up at her place later that evening, she would just have to impress upon him that she wanted to be left alone. She liked her nice, quiet, uneventful life. She had her charity work, her involvement with the TCC and the responsibility of running one of the largest horse ranches in Texas. The fulfillment of helping others and the enjoyment of raising her horses was enough for her. She didn't want or need the drama and tension that accompanied having a man around like Bradford Price.

Brad parked his newly purchased minivan in front of Abby's ranch house that evening, then got out and opened the sliding side door to unbuckle Sunnie's car seat. He still couldn't believe that he had bought the vehicle, let alone started driving it more than he did his Corvette. But now that he had a baby in his life, he found himself thinking of Sunnie's safety first. Trying to impress the ladies took a backseat to her welfare. Funny how someone so small could change his priorities so drastically, he thought as he smiled down at his sleeping niece.

Hanging the diaper bag on his shoulder, he took the carrier's handle in one hand, then picked up a bouquet of roses in the other. He owed Abby for all the help she had given him the past few days and although flowers didn't seem nearly enough to express how grateful he was to have her help last night, they would have to do for now. Once Juanita returned from Dallas, he would get her to watch Sunnie for an afternoon while he took Abby out for lunch.

Pleased with himself for thinking ahead, he climbed the porch steps and knocked on the front door. While he waited for Abby, he looked around. Although he and Richard Langley hadn't been especially good friends, Brad had been invited over for a few poker games with the guys throughout the years, and he could tell a big difference in the place since Abby moved in and put her stamp on it. Instead of the rustic wooden rocking chairs that Richard had preferred, a white wicker table and two matching chairs had been put in their place, and wind chimes hung on either end of the long, wide porch.

"What are you doing here, Brad?" Abby asked, opening the door.

"Didn't you find my note?" He knew for a fact that she had. Otherwise, he wouldn't have received the voice mail from her, telling him not to bother stopping by. "I left it under your windshield wiper."

"I found it." She folded her arms beneath her breasts as she stood, blocking the doorway. "Apparently you failed to get the message I left, telling you that I had made plans for the evening."

Smiling, he handed her the bouquet of roses. "Oh, I got it. But I promised Sunnie we would come over to thank you for all of your help the past few days, and I didn't want to disappoint her."

Brad knew he wasn't playing fair, considering Abby's fascination with the baby. But for reasons he didn't care to dwell on, he was the one who found himself disappointed at the prospect of not seeing Abby again. That alone should have been enough to send him running so far in the opposite direction that he crossed the border into Mexico before he stopped. But the truth was, he found that he enjoyed being with Abby. No other woman had ever challenged him the way she did. She kept him on his toes, and although he hadn't realized it, he had missed that when she was living in Seattle.

She stared at the peach-colored roses for a moment before she sighed and stepped back for him to enter the house. "I suppose I can put up my Christmas decorations tomorrow evening."

"There's no need to put it off." He waited for her to close the door behind him before setting the carrier down to remove his coat. Then, bending down, he pulled back the blanket he had draped over the baby. "Sunnie and I will be more than happy to help you put up the tree, string lights and do whatever else you want in the way of decorating."

She knelt down on the other side of the baby carrier and began unbuckling the safety straps. "That's all right. I can take care of it tomorrow."

"Actually, I'd really appreciate it if you'd let me help. It might give me some ideas about what I'm going to do for the holidays," he said truthfully.

"Haven't you decorated in the past?" she asked, frowning.

Shaking his head, Brad straightened to his full height. "Beyond buying a few gifts for my family, I really haven't taken the time to pay much attention to Christmas."

"And I'll bet your secretary did your shopping." Abby had guessed correctly. Her knowing look made him feel a bit guilty about his lack of attention to his gift giving.

"I gave her a price range and she took care of it for me," he admitted.

In hindsight, the least he could have done was to put a little thought into it and told his secretary what to buy. Hell, most of the time he hadn't even known what the woman had chosen until the recipient opened his gift.

"Now that you have Sunnie, you're going to have to start doing more to make the holidays special," Abby said, picking up the baby.

As they stood there eyeing each other, an idea began to form. He knew next to nothing about making Christmas a magical experience for a child, but he would bet every dime he had that Abby had thought about it—a lot.

"Will you help me?" he asked.

She frowned. "I'm sure Sadie would be more than happy to give you a few suggestions. After all, she has experience with what she's done for the twins."

He shook his head. "I want to start my own traditions with Sunnie, not copy what my sister does for her kids. Besides, now that she and Rick are married, it's their first Christmas together as a family. I don't want to intrude on that."

Abby was silent for several seconds as she seemed to think over what he had said. "I suppose that makes sense," she finally said, nodding. "But I'm not sure I'm the one you want to be giving you pointers on this."

"I am." Without a thought, he stepped closer. "Come

on, darlin'. Tell me you'll help me learn how to make Christmas all it should be for Sunnie."

Brad watched Abby close her eyes as if she struggled with her decision. When she opened them, she shook her head. "I wouldn't be doing this to help you. I'd be doing it for Sunnie."

"Of course," he said, careful to keep his tone from sounding triumphant. Whether it was for his or Sunnie's benefit, Abby was doing what he wanted, and he had the good sense not to draw attention to that fact.

He took a deep breath, then another. It was past time that he admitted what he'd been avoiding since kissing her under the mistletoe that day at the clubhouse. There was more than rivalry and teasing going on between them, and he was pretty sure she was as aware of it as he was. So what did he want to do about it? Was he ready to acknowledge that they had a chemistry between them that had quite possibly been there for most of their lives?

He wasn't sure. It could open up a whole can of worms that he would just as soon not deal with. He normally preferred women who weren't interested in anything more than a good time. But Abby never had been, nor would she ever be, that type. Abigail Langley was the type of woman who committed to a relationship, the type a man settled down with and raised a family.

Swallowing hard, he told himself to slow down. All he was asking for and all he wanted at the moment was her advice and help with his niece's first Christmas.

He leaned down to kiss Sunnie's cheek, then smiled at Abby. "So where do we start?"

"Start what?" she asked, looking distracted.

"Focus, Langley. You said you would help me with Christmas for Sunnie," he said, laughing. "I want to know where we should start."

Her cheeks colored a pretty pink. "For the record, I said if I helped it would be for Sunnie—not that I *would* help."

"But you will," he said. It wasn't a question, and he had no doubt that she was going to do it. He suspected her reticence had more to do with exercising a bit of the independence that was so much a part of her than any kind of reluctance to help him out.

She stared at him a moment longer, then sighing, she nodded. "Yes, I'll help you get ready for Sunnie's Christmas."

"Good." He picked up the empty baby carrier. "Now let's get this place decorated so we can start on mine. Where do you want the tree?"

"In front of the picture window in the living room," she said, heading in that direction.

As he followed her into the room, Brad couldn't wait to get her house finished so they could start on his place. He already had an idea of what he wanted to do, and if he was successful, it might very well prove to be one of the most enjoyable holiday seasons he'd had in a very long time.

Five

While Brad put the finishing touches on stringing the white twinkle lights around the front porch, Abby heated milk for two mugs of hot cocoa. She hadn't planned on doing much more than putting up a tree and maybe a wreath on the door, but as she opened each box of the decorations she had been collecting since childhood, her enthusiasm for the holidays grew.

It was amazing how much different this holiday season was from last year, she thought as she poured the milk into their cups. Newly widowed and dealing with the news that she would never have a family of her own, she hadn't had the heart to celebrate. But the passage of time had dulled the emotional pain of losing Richard, and although she still mourned her infertility, she was learning to deal with it.

"You can check 'lights around the outside of the

front windows' off your list," Brad said, walking into the kitchen. "What do you want me to put up next?"

"I think that's it." She dropped a spoonful of marsh-mallow cream into each mug, and turned to hand him his. "Is the baby still asleep?"

He nodded. "She seems to like sleeping in that carrier, but I'll be damned if I can figure out why." He took a sip of his cocoa. "It looks cramped to me."

"Why is it that as soon as some men sit in a reclining chair and put their feet up, they fall asleep?" she asked, smiling.

A frown creased his forehead. "I don't own one, but I guess most guys go to sleep in them because they're comfortable."

Laughing, she nodded as she walked back into the living room. "Just think of her carrier as a recliner for babies."

"I suppose that makes sense," he said, following her.

She sat down on the couch in front of the fireplace and looked around at their handiwork. "It's as pretty as I imagined it would be."

"You didn't decorate like this last year?" he asked, sitting down beside her.

Shaking her head, she shifted to face him. "Richard had just passed away a few weeks before the holidays, and I didn't want to be here alone for what should have been our first Christmas together as a married couple."

"I can understand that," Brad said, nodding. "Where did you go?"

"Back to Seattle." She shrugged one shoulder. "I still have my house on Lake Washington."

"How much shoreline do you have?" he asked, setting his mug on the end table.

"None." She grinned. "My house is *on* the lake."

He rested his arm along the back of the couch behind her. "Oh, you mean a houseboat like the one Tom Hanks lived in with his son in that movie several years ago?"

"They're called floating homes," she explained. "But my place isn't in as crowded of an area as the one in *Sleepless in Seattle.* I actually have a view that reminds me a lot of the lake where we used to go fishing when we were children."

A smile curved the corners of his mouth. "That was the first place I kissed you. Do you remember that?"

"How could I forget?" she asked, shuddering. "Right after that little peck on the lips you tried to put a grasshopper down the back of my shirt."

"If I remember correctly, you threatened to make me eat the damned thing if I did," he laughed.

She laughed with him. "And I would have, too." Taking a sip of her cocoa, she shook her head. "I'm surprised you remember that little incident."

They fell silent for a moment before she felt him lightly touch her hair. "That was the summer we were six years old and getting ready to go into the first grade," he said, his tone thoughtful. "Do you think that was what started our little game of one-upsmanship?"

"Maybe." She tried to recall when their rivalry began, but the sound of his rich voice and the feel of him stroking her hair distracted her. "I-it's so long ago, I'm not really certain when it began or why."

"Me, either." He threaded his fingers through her long curls. "But one thing's for sure—you've been driving me nuts for most of my life, Abigail Langley."

Her heart sped up as she met his piercing hazel gaze. "I'm sorry, but you've done your fair share of driving me to the brink, too."

"Don't be sorry." He cupped the back of her head with his hand to gently pull her forward. "There are different kinds of crazy, darlin'." His lips lightly brushed hers. "Right now, I'm thinking that it's the good kind."

Brad's mouth settled over hers, and Abby's eyes drifted shut. She wasn't so sure he was right about whether what was happening between them was good, but he was correct about one thing. It was definitely making her question her sanity. This was Brad Price, her lifelong nemesis and, most recently, her opponent for the presidency of the Texas Cattleman's Club. He was the very last man she should be kissing. But heaven help her, she couldn't seem to find the will to stop him.

When he pulled her against him and deepened the kiss, her heart skipped several beats and she abandoned all thought. The feel of his wide chest pressed against her breasts, and the tingling excitement of his tongue stroking her inner recesses, sent a wave of heat spiraling through every part of her. She had missed the intimacy of having a man's strong arms around her, of tasting the desire in his kiss. Without a thought to the consequences, she brought her arms up to wrap them around his shoulders as she gave in to the temptation of once again feeling cherished by a man.

Moving his hand, Brad cupped her breast and worried the hardened tip with the pad of his thumb. Even through her clothing, the sensations he created caused a spiraling surge of need that stole her breath.

She suddenly felt weightless, and it took a moment for her to realize that Brad had lifted her to sit on his lap. Melting against him, she could have easily lost herself in the moment had it not been for the feel of his rapidly changing body against the side of her hip and the answering ache of emptiness settling deep within her.

He wanted her and she wanted him. The realization was enough to send panic sweeping through her and immediately helped to clear her head.

"I—I think…I'll go make us another cup of… cocoa," she said breathlessly, pulling away from him.

His smile meaningful, he shook his head. "Cocoa isn't what I want."

Abby's heart fluttered wildly at his low, intimate tone. "That's all I'm offering, Brad."

"For now," he said, nodding. "But that doesn't mean the door is permanently closed on the subject." Before she could tell him differently, he gave her a quick kiss and set her on the couch beside him, then stood up. "I think it's time for Sunnie and I to call it a night. What time do you want to go shopping tomorrow?"

The speed at which he switched topics made her head spin. "What are you talking about? I didn't mention anything about going shopping with you."

"I told you I've never bothered to decorate before and I don't have anything," he said, pulling her up from the couch. Placing his hands on her shoulders, he smiled. "We have to pick out a tree, get ornaments and lights and whatever else you think I need."

"I could give you a list," she offered, desperately trying to think of an excuse not to help him.

"Nope." He smiled as he turned to arrange blankets over his sleeping niece in the baby carrier. "It would be best for you to go with me."

"I'd rather not," she said, shaking her head.

He stopped getting the baby ready to leave and turned to face her. "Why?"

How could she explain that the more time she spent with him and the baby, the more time she wanted to spend? How it reminded her of all the things she wanted but would never have?

When she hesitated a little too long, he smiled. "I'll be by around noon to pick you up." He gave her a kiss that curled her toes inside her fuzzy slippers, then picked up the baby and walked to the door. "We'll grab a bite of lunch and then hit the mall. See you tomorrow, darlin'."

Rendered speechless by his kiss, Abby simply watched the door close behind him. What on earth was wrong with her? Why was it that all Brad had to do was kiss her and she lost control of her thought processes and did what he wanted? And why was she letting him kiss her in the first place?

She had never been a pushover in her entire life. In fact, she had been accused of being the exact opposite on numerous occasions. Her mother had always told her she was a little too self-reliant for her own good, and even Richard had complained that at times he didn't think she needed him as much as he needed her.

Sinking back down on the couch, she stared at her

Christmas tree. What was it about Bradford Price that caused her to act so out of character?

From the time they were children just the thought of being around him caused her to feel edgy and anxious, as if she were waiting for…something. But what? A gesture? A move to let her know how he felt about her?

Her heart slammed into her ribs and she had to struggle to draw her next breath. Had what she thought was a spirited rivalry all these years actually been a mask for the attraction that was only now boiling to the surface?

Ridiculous. She took a deep, steadying breath. There had to be a perfectly good explanation for what was happening between her and Brad.

Most likely it was the combination of her wanting a baby but not being able to have one and him having just gained custody of his niece. Couple that with the fact that they were the only two single members of their circle of friends, and it was only natural that they would gravitate toward each other.

Satisfied that she had discovered the reason for what was happening between them, she rose to her feet and started toward the stairs leading up to her bedroom. Now that she had solved the mystery, she felt ready to deal with the situation. The first thing tomorrow morning, she would call and cancel their excursion to the mall, then she fully intended to throw herself into helping Sadie with plans for her family cultural center, as well as doubling her volunteer work at the women's shelter.

Changing into her night shirt, Abby pulled back the

comforter and climbed into bed. As long as she stayed busy and kept her distance from Brad and his adorable little niece, she would be just fine.

"Good morning," Brad said as soon as Sadie answered the phone. "How is my favorite little sister?"

"Suspicious," she answered without the least bit of hesitation. "What do you want, Brad?"

"I didn't mention wanting anything," he said, grinning as he spooned a bit of cereal into Sunnie's eager little mouth.

"You didn't have to," Sadie said, laughing. "Your choice of greetings tells me that you're up to something. What do you need?"

He wasn't the least bit surprised that his sister had figured out there had to be a motive behind his early-morning call. She knew him better than anyone else, and at times he suspected she might know him better than he knew himself.

"Could you watch Sunnie this afternoon for a couple of hours?" he asked, anticipating her affirmative answer.

"Of course," she said, just as he thought she would. "The twins will love spending time with their baby cousin."

"Great." He wiped a smear of cereal from Sunnie's chin. "I'll bring her over a little before noon."

"Are you having lunch with one of your clients?" Sadie asked conversationally.

"No, I'm taking Abby to lunch before we go shopping for Christmas decorations." He tucked the phone between his ear and shoulder as he lifted the baby from the high chair. "Abby is helping me get ready for Sunnie's first Christmas." Dead silence followed his announcement. "Sadie, are you still there?"

"Yes."

"Okay, what do you have against Abby and I spending time together?" He knew Sadie wouldn't comment unless asked.

"Actually, I don't have anything against it," she said, sounding as if she weighed each word carefully. She hesitated a moment before she continued, "I just don't want to see Abby get hurt."

"I'm not about to hurt Abby," he said, frowning. "What gives you the idea that I would?"

He heard her sigh. "I know you wouldn't mean to do it, but let's face it, you have a 'love 'em and leave 'em' reputation. And whether deserved or not, you'll have to admit you've dated a lot of women with absolutely no thought of commitment."

There was no way he could refute what his sister said. He had seen his share of the ladies over the past ten years, but it wasn't as if he had led them on. They had all known right up front that he wasn't interested in anything more than the pleasure of their company for an evening or two.

"Abby and I are friends." He walked into the family room to put Sunnie in her swing. "She's been helping me figure out things with the baby."

"Bradford Price, don't feed me a line," Sadie said, her tone stern. "For one thing, you and Abby have never been friends."

"We're both competitive and have been for as long

as either one of us can remember, but we've never been sworn enemies, either," he said in his own defense.

"I suppose that's true," Sadie said, sounding thoughtful. "But if you'll remember, I witnessed that kiss you gave her the other morning. That wasn't a gesture of friendship. It was more like the prelude to seduction."

He wasn't about to insult his sister's intelligence by denying that the kiss had been passionate. But he didn't want to discuss the motive behind it, when he wasn't exactly certain what it was.

"Sadie, I give you my word that I would never intentionally do anything to upset Abby or cause her any kind of emotional pain," he assured her.

"Thank you, Brad." They were both silent for a moment before Sadie spoke again. "Just be extremely careful not to hurt her, even unintentionally. I know I'm being overly protective, but she's my best friend, and the past year has been terribly rough for her. I just think it's time she experienced some happiness in her life."

Brad couldn't fault his sister for being loyal to a friend. It was one of the traits he admired most about her.

"Abby is lucky to have you on her side," he said, meaning it.

For some time after their call ended, Brad stood in the middle of the family room staring at the phone he still held. The last thing in the world he wanted to do was cause Abby any kind of distress. Maybe it would be in both of their best interests if he backed off and let her go her way while he went his.

But he rejected that train of thought almost as soon as it came to mind. He had no idea why he felt so compelled to spend time with Abby, why he wanted to hold her in his arms, kiss her until they both gasped for breath and more, but he did. And although she was doing her best to fight it, he suspected that she was experiencing the same magnetic pull he was.

Considering it was the first time in his life he felt that way about any woman, he owed it to both of them to take the time to find out what was going on. He had always believed that life was full of possibilities, and passing one up might very well mean a missed opportunity. And for reasons he couldn't quite put his finger on, he sensed that this was one chance that was important enough not to miss.

Abby couldn't believe she was standing in the Royal Diner with Brad, waiting to be seated. She had tried calling him several times throughout the morning to cancel their shopping trip, and even left a message on his voice mail telling him to count her out. Unfortunately he either failed to check his messages or simply ignored them. She suspected the latter, but when he showed up on her doorstep at noon, he denied knowing anything about it.

"Would you rather sit at a table or in one of the booths?" he asked, leaning close.

A shiver streaked straight up her spine at the feel of his warm breath feathering over her ear. "A…booth," she answered, cursing the breathless tone of her voice.

"There's an empty booth in the corner," he said,

placing his hand to the small of her back to guide her to the far side of the diner.

Thankful the table would be between them, Abby quickly slid into one side of the booth. When she noticed a couple of TCC members sitting across the room, their curious gazes fixed on her and Brad, it was all she could do not to groan aloud.

"I don't think this was a good idea," she said, picking up one of the menus left by a passing waitress.

"Why do you say that?" he asked, frowning. "I thought everyone in town liked the food here."

"It's not that I don't like the food." Apparently he hadn't noticed the attention they were getting. "I think Travis Whelan and David Sorensen are going to choke on their chili at the sight of the two of us together."

Instead of being subtle about looking over at the two men, Brad turned to call out a greeting. "Hey, Trav. Dave. How are things going?"

"Can't complain," Travis said, smiling.

"Are you two ready for the Christmas Ball and the announcement of the new TCC officers?" David asked.

"About as ready as we'll ever be," Brad said, smiling.

Travis nodded. "Good luck to both of you."

"Thank you," Abby said, wanly.

Great. Just what she needed. By the end of the day, the entire membership of the Texas Cattleman's Club would be speculating about the fact that she and Brad were seen having lunch together.

"What's wrong?" Brad asked, frowning.

She sighed. There were times men could be so clueless. "In case you hadn't noticed, we just supplied the rumor mill with enough grist to last until the ball next week."

"Is that all?" He laughed. "I doubt that our having lunch together will be cause for any kind of gossip."

"You're kidding, right?" She stared at him in disbelief. "It's been a well-known fact for the past several months that you didn't even want me to gain membership to the club, let alone run for president."

His easy expression faded. "I'm not denying that I wanted the club to remain the way it's been since its inception. But that doesn't mean I haven't accepted that the majority of the membership saw it differently when they voted to honor the bylaws and let you in." He reached across the table to cover her hand with his. "Relax, darlin'. If anyone asks, we're just two club members having lunch together. Hell, they might even speculate that we're trying to bridge the gap between the old guard and the newer TCC members."

What Brad said made sense, but it was hard to concentrate with his hand engulfing hers. "I suppose you're right," she finally managed. "I just hate being the hot topic for all of the gossips in town until the next scandal comes along for them to dissect. I've been there before and once was enough to last me a lifetime."

His frown told her that he had no idea what she was talking about. "I don't recall you ever doing anything that would cause the gossips' tongues to start wagging."

"I didn't. But I can't say the same about my father." It had been sixteen years ago but Abby still cringed when she thought about dealing with the aftermath he had left behind.

"You mean when your dad left you and your mom?" Brad asked gently.

She nodded. "I hated having people suddenly stop talking when I walked into a room or catching them stare at me while they whispered to each other."

"I can understand that." He lightly squeezed her hand. "But the best way to combat that is to act as if nothing is going on." He looked thoughtful a moment before he spoke again. "I think as a show of solidarity, we should plan on attending the Christmas Ball together."

She stared at him, then laughed out loud. "You've lost your mind, haven't you?"

"Probably, but I think it would send a message to the membership that we have nothing to hide and that no matter who wins the presidency, we're willing to work together." Grinning, he shrugged. "People are going to talk no matter what we do, and that's just a fact of life, darlin'. But if we act as if nothing out of the ordinary is going on, they quickly lose interest."

"You're serious," she said incredulously.

"Yup." He released her hand and picked up his menu as if she had already agreed to his harebrained idea. "I'm going to have the chili. What would you like?"

"I, um, guess I'll have the chef salad," Abby said, unable to get her mind off of his plan for them to attend the ball together.

As Brad gave the waitress their order, Abby had to admit that she could understand his reasoning. If they went together to the annual event, it would definitely send a clear message to the general membership that no matter which one of them took over leadership of the prestigious club, they intended to put the past behind them and work to heal the rift that had threatened the club in the past several months. But the way he said it made it sound too much like a date for her peace of mind.

"I suppose I could meet you there and then we could sit at the same table," she said, after the waitress walked toward the kitchen to turn in their order.

"Not acceptable," he said, shaking his head. "I'll pick you up and we'll go together."

"I don't think that would be—"

"You're overthinking this, Abby," he interrupted her. "It doesn't send a strong enough message if we just sit together. Hell, they'll probably seat us at the same table anyway. All you have to do is tell me what time I should pick you up."

She couldn't argue with what he said. All of the candidates for the various offices and their guests would most likely be sitting at a handful of tables in the front of the room. But how on earth did she manage to get into situations like this? More important, how was she going to get out of it?

"I'll give it some thought," she said, avoiding a definite answer. She had a week or so before the ball. Surely she could come up with a plausible reason why they should drive to the ball separately.

When the waitress returned with their food, then moved to the next table, Brad smiled. "Now that we have that settled, I think we had better eat and get this shopping trip underway. I promised Sadie that we wouldn't be gone long." He chuckled. "By the time we get back there, she'll probably be tearing her hair from taking care of three kids under the age of three."

Having so many little ones to take care of sounded like heaven to Abby. "You'll have to give your sister a break and babysit for her sometime," she said, smiling.

She couldn't help but laugh at his horrified expression. "That sounds like a recipe for disaster. There are times I'm still not entirely certain of what to do for Sunnie. I can't imagine adding a couple of toddlers to the mix." He frowned. "I would definitely need help."

Abby took a bite of her salad and chewed thoughtfully. "Maybe when your housekeeper returns from Dallas, you can get her to volunteer."

He shook his head. "Number one, Juanita doesn't volunteer for anything. I'd have to pay her. And number two, I doubt there's enough money in the state of Texas to tempt her into agreeing to watch three babies at once." He took a sip of his iced tea. "You're good with kids. You could help."

"I didn't say anything about—"

"Don't think you can handle it, Langley?" he asked, his hazel gaze capturing hers.

There was just enough challenge in his tone to put her on the defensive. "I'm sure I could handle it better than you."

"Then let's put it to a test," he suggested. "When we pick up Sunnie, I'll tell Sadie that we'll babysit while she and Rick go out tomorrow evening."

Abby opened her mouth to decline, but the combination of Brad's challenge and the temptation of spending time with the adorable twin girls and the sweet baby who had captured her heart were more than she could resist. Besides, weekends seemed to drag on interminably for her, and taking care of children would be a welcomed relief from the most boring part of the week.

"All right." She smiled. "Challenge accepted. We'll see just who loses a handful of their hair first."

A mischievous look crossed his handsome face. "Let's make this interesting."

"What do you…have in mind?" she asked hesitantly. What was he up to this time?

"At the end of the evening, whoever complains first about being tired or even yawns has to make dinner for the other." He looked so self-assured she almost laughed.

"You do realize you're going to lose, don't you?"

"Oh, I'm not so sure about that, Langley," he said, sounding quite confident. "We'll just see who's left standing when the dust settles."

"Yes, we most certainly will," she agreed, relishing the challenge.

Her competitive nature had come to full alert and it was game on. She was really going to enjoy watching the indomitable Mr. Price eat crow when he learned that taking care of children was the one thing she would never get tired of.

Three hours after driving Abby home and picking Sunnie up from his sister's place, Brad found himself pulling every Christmas decoration known to God and man from the mountain of shopping bags on his family room floor. He was searching for the one filled with mistletoe.

"I know it's here," he muttered.

When he finally found the plastic bag with enough mistletoe to decorate half the town of Royal, he grinned. By the time Abby showed up tonight, he fully intended to have the most important part of his decorating complete.

Checking on the baby to make sure she was still napping, he grabbed the small box of pushpins from the desk in his study and started to work. Twenty minutes later, just as he finished hanging the last sprig of the greenery, the doorbell rang.

"Right on time," he said, opening the door.

"Time for what?" Abby asked, frowning.

"Come in and I'll show you." He took her by the arm and led her into the middle of the foyer. "Look up, darlin'."

When she glanced up at the chandelier, she shook her head. "Of all the things you could have decorated, you chose to start with hanging mistletoe over putting up the tree?"

Taking her into his arms, he kissed her chin. "It's the most important decoration of all."

"Oh, really? By whose definition?" she asked, putting a bit of space between them.

"Mine," he said, brushing her lips with his. She wasn't pushing away from him, and as long as he kept her off guard, there was a chance she wouldn't. "It's one of the oldest of holiday traditions. For something to be around for a couple of hundred years or more, it has to be significant."

"When did you decide this?" she asked, sounding a little breathless.

"I think the first time I realized mistletoe's importance was over a week ago at the TCC clubhouse," he said, pulling her a little closer. "When I kissed you."

He watched her nervously moisten her lips. "This isn't wise, Brad."

"Why?" he asked, enjoying the feel of her slender form within the circle of his arms. "I like kissing you and you like being kissed. Where's the harm in that?"

"I…" She caught her lower lip with her teeth as if she were trying to find the right words. "I can't be what you want me to be."

Noticing that she hadn't denied she liked having him kiss her, Brad brought his hand up to brush her dark auburn hair from her soft cheek. "What do you think that is, Abby?"

"I'm not…entirely sure." She took a deep breath. "But I know what I can't be. I can't be one of your casual affairs. That's just not me. That's not who I am."

"I know that, darlin'." Threading his fingers through her silky waves, he gently pulled her closer. "All I want is for you to be who you've always been—Abby Langley, the woman who has challenged me to be the best I can be all of my life and recently became a good friend."

Before she could speculate further on what she thought he wanted from her, Brad lowered his mouth to hers. He didn't want to think about where their friendship was going or why kissing her was quickly becoming an obsession for him. He had a feeling he wouldn't be overly comfortable with what might be one of the most meaningful realizations of his life.

The moment their lips met, heat spread throughout

his body. Without a second thought, he deepened the kiss to once again lose himself in the sweetness that was uniquely Abby. He moved to take her hands in his and raise them to his shoulders, giving him free access to her full breasts. Covering the soft mounds with his palms, he felt the tips bead in eager anticipation, and his body answered with an urgent tightening of its own.

He would have liked nothing more than to feel Abby's much softer skin pressed to his, to hear her sigh of pleasure as he sank himself deep inside of her. But aside from the fact that the barrier of their clothing prevented that from happening, she wasn't yet ready to take that step, and he had never been a man to push for more than a woman was willing to give. Hell, he wasn't entirely certain he was ready for that step himself.

As if on cue, the sound of Sunnie's awakening for a bottle came through the speaker on the baby monitor, adding one more reason for him to break the kiss.

Brad regretfully raised his head to stare down into Abby's dazed blue eyes. "While I get the baby's bottle ready, why don't you go up to the nursery before she really gets wound up?"

Abby stared at him for several seconds before she nodded and turned to go upstairs. But he felt rooted to the spot. The sight of her blue-jeans-clad bottom swaying enticingly as she ascended the steps was driving him crazy, and it wasn't until she had disappeared down the hall at the top of the stairs that he forced himself to move.

There was no doubt about it. He and Abby would

eventually take that next step and become lovers. He just hoped he didn't end up going completely crazy before they did.

Six

Cradling Sunnie in one arm, Abby pointed to the lights Brad had just wound around the Christmas tree. "If you leave those there, you're going to have a bare spot with no lights at all on the other side."

"I probably should have bought another string of them," he said, moving the lights around to cover the area she had pointed out.

When he finished, she eyed the rearrangement. "For all of your grumbling, it looks good," she said, smiling. "Now you need to start hanging the ornaments."

"Aren't you going to help with that?" he asked, reaching for a box of silver balls. "It was your idea that I get a tree this big. The least you could do is get in on some of the fun."

Abby ignored his sarcastic tone. She was perfectly content to direct the project while holding Sunnie. "I've been having fun taking care of this little angel," she said, staring down at the sweet baby girl in her arms. "She's fascinated with all of this activity."

Brad stepped over a pile of garland to come over and tickle Sunnie's tummy. "We're doing all of this for you, munchkin. I hope you appreciate it."

The baby squealed with delight as she reached for Brad's hand.

Abby could tell the baby adored him, and her chest tightened from the knowledge that she would never experience that kind of love from a child. "I think I'll put Sunnie in her swing and make a couple of mugs of cocoa while you finish putting the ornaments on the tree," she said, suddenly needing a few minutes to herself.

"That sounds good." He glanced at his watch. "I'd like to get this done so we can relax for a few minutes before I have to get Sunnie in bed for the night."

Nodding, Abby put the baby in her swing, then went into Brad's kitchen. Leaning against the counter, she closed her eyes as she fought to keep the emotions building inside of her at bay.

The life she wanted, had always dreamed about having for as long as she could remember, was just in the other room. But it wasn't hers. She was just a guest Brad had asked to help him get ready for his first Christmas with the baby—the outsider looking in at what she wanted with all of her heart, but could never have.

She took a deep breath, swiped at the lone tear slowly making its way down her cheek and forced herself to move. Throwing herself a pity party was counterproductive and a waste of time and energy. A family of her own was never going to be hers, and she might as well get used to it.

Composing herself while she prepared the cocoa, she decided to make her excuses and leave as soon as possible. It made absolutely no sense to stay around and torture herself. Sunnie was not her child to love and care for, and Brad, with his killer kisses and sexy charm, could quickly become an addiction for which she strongly suspected there wasn't a cure. And that was something she wanted to avoid at all costs.

It was definitely in her best interest to back away from the situation and let Brad and his niece form their little family unit without her. If she didn't, she could very well become too attached to both of them and end up getting her heart broken. That was something she couldn't let happen. Her survival depended on it.

By the time she walked back into the family room with the steaming mugs, Abby felt a little more in control and ready to distance herself from temptation. "Where's Sunnie?" she asked, immediately noticing the baby wasn't in her swing.

"I put her in her crib upstairs," Brad said, taking the mug Abby handed him. "I guess the combination of the swing's motion and watching me wrestle with that damned garland was boring enough to put her to sleep."

"Well, bah humbug to you, too, Mr. Scrooge," Abby said, gazing at his handiwork. "Whether you liked doing it or not, you did a good job. Everything looks very nice."

"Thanks." He took her mug from her, then placing

both cups on the end table, gathered her into his arms. "I couldn't have done it without your help, darlin'."

Her heart beat double time, and every one of her good intentions evaporated like mist in the morning sun. She might have been able to cling to her resolve had he not touched her. But the feel of his strength surrounding her and the lull of his deep baritone caused her to forget the importance of putting distance between them.

"I'm sure you could have managed," she said, trying to find the will to pull away from him.

"Probably, but it wouldn't have been nearly as much fun," he whispered close to her ear.

Tingles of excitement skipped over every nerve in her body and she had to remind herself to breathe. "You had fun grumbling about the lights and the garland?"

His deep chuckle vibrated against her breasts. "I'll let you in on a secret. I grumble about a lot things that I really don't mind doing."

Feeling as if the tendons in her legs had been replaced with rubber bands, Abby wrapped her arms around his waist to support herself. "W-why?"

"It's a guy thing." He nuzzled his cheek against hers. "It's expected of us."

Closing her eyes, Abby couldn't stop herself from leaning into his touch. "What else is expected of you?"

"This," he said as his mouth brushed over hers.

He nibbled at her lips without really kissing her, and she couldn't believe the level of tension building inside of her. More than anything, she wanted him to deepen the caress and allow her to once again experience his passion.

"Do you want me to kiss you, Abby?" he asked, as he continued his tender teasing.

She knew she shouldn't, but that was exactly what she wanted. "Y-yes."

When he finally settled his mouth over hers, then parted her lips with his tongue to deepen the kiss, Abby felt as if the earth moved. The level of anticipation, the desperate need that Brad created, was unlike anything she had ever experienced.

Lights flashed behind her closed eyes as his tongue grazed hers, then engaged her in a game of advance and retreat. If she had thought his kisses were intoxicating before, they were but a mere glimpse of the erotic expertise he was showing her now.

Forgetting all of the reasons she should pull out of his arms and run back to the sanctuary of her ranch, she shamelessly pressed herself more fully against his lower body at the same time she tugged his T-shirt from the waistband of his jeans. There would be plenty of time later to regret her recklessness. At the moment, all she could do—all she wanted to do—was feel. She wanted to once again feel cherished. Needed to feel desired. And she craved the feel of his hard body inside of hers.

"I can't believe...I'm going to say this...darlin'," Brad said, sounding completely out of breath. He reached down to catch her hands in his. "But we need... to slow this...down."

It took a moment for Abby to realize what he had said. When she did, it was as effective as taking a plunge into a pool of icy water.

What on earth had she done? Why had she let go of the tight control that was so much a part of her?

Humiliated and unable to think of anything to say that would even come close to explaining her wanton actions, she remained silent. Pulling away from Brad, she refused to look at him as she rushed down the hall to the foyer closet. She needed to go home, crawl into bed and pray that when she awoke in the morning, she would find that she hadn't let her guard down and made a fool of herself with Brad, that it had all been a bad dream.

"Abby, where the hell do you think you're going?" Brad called, following close behind.

When his large hands came down on her shoulders, he turned her to face him and Abby made a point of fixing her gaze on the ribbed collar of his T-shirt. "H-home," she stammered. "I...need to get home."

"Why?"

She tried to back away from him. "I...just do."

"No, you don't." He applied just enough pressure to keep her firmly in place without hurting her. "You need to stay right here and talk to me. Do you have any idea why I called a halt to that kiss?"

Why wouldn't he let it go? Couldn't he at least let her keep a small scrap of her dignity?

"I don't think you have to put it into words," she said, shaking her head.

She still hadn't looked him directly in the eye and she wasn't sure she could. The well-respected, extremely independent Abigail Langley had never in her life let go and lost control of herself with any man—not even with her late husband.

"Look at me, Abby," he commanded. When she continued to stare at his chest, he placed his forefinger beneath her chin and raised her head to meet his gaze. "The reason I stopped you wasn't because I don't want you. Right now, I'm hard as hell and would like nothing more than to carry you up the stairs and spend the entire night loving you the way you were meant to be loved. But you're not ready for that." He gave her a kiss so tender she had to blink back tears. "When we make love, it's going to be long and slow, and the next morning there won't be any regrets."

Abby's heart skipped a beat at the determination in his piercing hazel eyes. What was she supposed to say to that? What could she say?

Thanking him for keeping her from making a fool of herself or for telling her that he intended to make love to her the way she'd never been made love to before was inappropriate and would be humiliating beyond words.

"I, um…really should go, Brad," she finally managed to say.

He kissed her forehead, then hugged her close. "I'll see you tomorrow evening, darlin'."

"I don't think—"

"Hush, Abby," he said, placing one finger to her lips. He gave her a smile that left her insides feeling like warm pudding. "We'll have three kids to chaperone us."

She had forgotten about babysitting for Rick and Sadie and didn't feel that she could back out of helping Brad. Her conscience wouldn't allow her to leave him to care for three children by himself when he was adjusting to taking care of one, nor did she want to keep her best friend from spending some much-needed alone time with her husband.

Resigned, she nodded. "I'll see you tomorrow."

"I'll be looking forward to it," he said, giving her a smile that could melt the polar ice caps.

Shrugging into her jacket, she simply walked to the door and left. There was no point in trying to argue with him that the more time they spent together, the more dangerous the situation became for her. He wouldn't listen anyway. Besides, she needed to analyze her uncharacteristic behavior. She needed to figure out why she had so easily let herself go with Brad when she hadn't even been able to be that free with Richard.

Once she had the answer, she had every intention of shoring up her defenses to prevent it from happening again. If she didn't, there was a very real possibility she would end up falling for Brad.

And make an even bigger fool of herself than she had tonight.

"I took the liberty of ordering for both of us," Sadie said when Abby hurried over to where she sat in a booth at the Royal Diner.

"Sorry I'm late." Abby slid across the red and white vinyl seat on the other side of the booth. "After you called this morning about meeting for lunch, my foreman sent for me to go down to the barn because one of my mares went into labor sometime during the night. She didn't give birth until about an hour ago."

"I hope everything went well." Sadie smiled. She waited for the waitress to set their plates in front of them and move on to another table before she asked, "Did the mare have a little stud or a filly?"

"Filly," Abby said, happily. "I had a special name picked out and it wouldn't have sounded right if the foal had been a stud."

Her friend laughed. "Well, don't keep me in suspense. What are you going to name her?"

"Sunnie's Moonlight Dancer is the name she'll be registered under with the American Quarter Horse Association," Abby explained. "But around the ranch we'll call her Dancer."

"You named her after the baby?" Her glass of iced tea half-way to her mouth, Sadie stopped to give her a questioning look.

"I thought it sounded pretty," Abby said, placing her paper napkin in her lap. "Besides, when Sunnie's old enough, I plan on giving Dancer to her."

There wasn't a question of whether the baby would grow up riding horses. Everyone in and around Royal either had a horse or knew how to ride one.

"It's very pretty." Looking thoughtful, Sadie set her glass back on the table. "You've fallen in love with my brother and niece, haven't you?"

Abby's heart stopped for several beats as a jolting panic coursed through her. She couldn't dispute caring deeply for the baby. But Brad? Was that why she always gave in to his insistence that he needed her help with this or that? Could that be the reason she lost all will to resist whenever he held her, kissed her?

No, definitely not. She couldn't—wouldn't—allow herself to love anyone else. It was too risky, would be too painful if she lost them the way she had lost Richard—or the baby she had tried to adopt, only to have the mother change her mind.

"N-no. I mean, of course I think the world of Sunnie. Who doesn't? But Brad? No, definitely not." She knew she was babbling, but couldn't seem to stop herself. "He's nice enough, but…well, no, I don't love him. We're just friends."

"Of course you don't," Sadie said smugly.

Abby could tell by the look on her best friend's face that she didn't believe a word Abby had just said. "No, really. I like Brad, but we're just friends."

Sadie nodded. "That's why the two of you have been almost inseparable for the past week."

"I'm just helping him get ready for Sunnie's first Christmas," Abby heard herself saying defensively. She knew she was beginning to sound like a broken record, but she couldn't think of any other plausible excuse.

"You don't have to explain yourself to me, Abby." Sadie's smile was filled with understanding. "I'm not condemning you. Heaven knows, I was a complete wreck when Rick and I were trying to sort out everything."

"I'm so very glad it worked out for the two of you," Abby said, meaning it. "But there's nothing going on between—"

"Save it." Sadie laughed. "I've heard that song before. I don't need to hear it again." Her expression turned serious. "I didn't invite you to lunch to quiz you on your feelings for my brother."

"Why did you want to meet with me?" Abby asked curiously. Normally when they had lunch together it was planned well in advance due to Sadie's need to find a sitter.

"Actually there are a couple of things." Sadie took a sip of her tea. "I've made a couple of decisions about the family cultural and community center I want to run by you."

Much more comfortable with the topic of conversation, Abby picked up her fork. "What have you decided?"

"I want it to be a place where families can not only expose their children to the arts, but also receive the help they need in times of crisis." Her friend looked thoughtful. "Times are tough for a lot of people right now, and I want them to have a place to go when they have a shortfall and find that they need assistance with things like utility bills or a month's rent."

"I think that's a wonderful idea. Let me know when and where to volunteer." Abby took a bite of her salad. "Where do you plan on putting it? Are you still hoping the TCC will donate their clubhouse if they vote to build a new one, or are you going to try to find some land and start fresh?"

"I'm still hoping for the clubhouse," Sadie said, staring into space as if imagining the possibilities the building afforded. "It really has everything I need—office space, a ballroom that could easily be turned into an auditorium for concerts and art exhibits, as well as the gym for physical activities. But if that doesn't happen, I'll explore building."

Abby nodded enthusiastically. "I'm hoping you get the clubhouse. I think it would be ideal." They fell silent a moment before she asked, "What was the other thing you wanted to discuss with me?"

Sadie looked a bit hesitant. "Some of the TCC members have been talking," she said slowly. "Rick told me that several of them have asked him what's going on with you and Brad spending so much time together."

Abby's heart sank. She had warned Brad it would happen when they were seen having lunch together just the day before.

"What did Rick tell them?" she asked, rubbing at the tension headache suddenly building at her temples.

"You know how Rick is. He politely but firmly told them that if they worried more about what was going on in their own lives, they wouldn't have time to wonder about others." Sadie smiled. "Actually, I think he was a little more graphic when he talked to them, but that's the gist of what he said."

Groaning, Abby pushed her plate away from her. Ravenous when she had arrived, she suddenly found that her appetite had deserted her. "I appreciate that he put them in their places, but I hate being gossiped about."

"I know what that's like," Sadie said, nodding. "If you'll remember back about five months ago, Rick and I were the talk of the town."

"That's the one thing about living in Seattle that I miss more than anything else." She sighed wistfully. "It's big enough that no one knows or cares who your friends are or what you're doing."

"Gossip is one of the hazards of living in a small town, that's for sure," Sadie agreed. "But I thought you should be aware of it."

"Thanks." Truthfully, she wasn't sure if she wouldn't have been better off being blissfully unaware. At least, she wouldn't have felt like everyone was whispering about her when she walked into a room.

"There's one other thing I wanted to ask you about," Sadie said, placing her paper napkin on the table. "Are you and Brad sure you want to babysit this evening?"

"Of course." Even though being with Brad was going to be a bit awkward after last night, she couldn't disappoint her friend. "I'm looking forward to it. You know how much I love your girls."

Sadie looked relieved. "Thanks. I would really like to spend some quality time with my husband. Alone."

"I don't blame you," Abby said. "Brad and I actually have a little wager on who will tire out first—me or him."

"Oh, sweetie, you've seen the girls in action. I think you and Brad will both be wiped out by the end of the evening." Sadie grinned. "By the way, what's the prize?"

"Whoever loses has to make dinner for the other one." Abby laughed for the first time since learning she and Brad were the hot topic in Royal. "I have every intention of being the winner on this one."

"You go, girlfriend," Sadie said, checking her watch. She tossed a few dollars on the table for the waitress, then gathered her purse and jacket. "I've got to run. One of the neighbors down the way from us woke up with the pink flamingos in his yard this morning. He was on his way to Houston on business and asked me to take his donation to the women's shelter to get rid of them."

"Don't blame me for that one," Abby said, laughing. "I've helped put them in people's yards a few times, but I have no idea who all is on the list."

Sadie shrugged one shoulder. "I really don't mind. It's for a good cause. But the sooner that I make Mr. Higgins's donation, the sooner they can be put in someone else's yard and make more money for the shelter."

"I expect to see them in my yard any day," Abby said, sliding out of the booth.

"Rick and I will bring the girls over to Brad's place around seven this evening," Sadie said, as they walked toward the cashier at the end of the lunch counter.

"That sounds good." After paying for their lunch, Abby followed Sadie outside. "But I thought we would be watching them at your house."

Her friend shook her head as they walked across the parking lot. "The twins will probably still be awake when we get back, but I'm sure Sunnie will be asleep. I thought it would be easier for you to go ahead and put her to bed for the night, instead of having to get her up to bring her home."

"You're probably right," Abby said, giving her friend a hug. "I'll see you tonight at Brad's."

On the drive back to her ranch, Abby couldn't help but think about what Sadie had told her. The last thing she had wanted was to once again be the talk of the TCC membership. Some of the older members had been downright outraged when she decided to run for the office of president and still grumbled about her admittance into the prestigious club. Now that the actual voting had taken place, things seemed to have died down a bit as they awaited the election results. That was just the way she wanted it to stay, too.

She was going to have to discuss the matter with Brad and tell him that attending the ball together was definitely off the table. She had been looking for an excuse not to go with him, anyway, and this was as good as any. There was no way she wanted to attend the event with him and cause the rumors to escalate. Now all she had to do was get that point across to him.

Abby sighed. She most definitely had her work cut out for her. If there was one thing she had learned in the past couple of weeks, it was that Brad Price was about as determined to have his way as anyone she had ever met.

Abby smiled as she sat in the rocking chair, giving Sunnie a bottle while she observed Brad interacting with his nieces, Wendy and Gail. After pretending he was a pony and crawling around on the floor giving them rides, helping them build towers of blocks to knock over and holding a stuffed bunny for the girls to feed pretend food to, he was seated on the couch with one snuggled close on either side of him. They were watching a classic Disney cartoon on a DVD that Sadie had brought over with them and he seemed just as focused on the television as the girls were.

She could tell Wendy and Gail adored their uncle and he returned their feelings. Every time one of them pointed out something that happened on the television, Brad gave her his full attention and acted as if what she told him was of the utmost importance. He was going to be a wonderful father to Sunnie and any other children he would eventually have.

Abby's chest tightened with emotion at the thought that she wouldn't be a part of it all. There were no nights spent watching classic children's shows with toddlers in her future, no rocking babies to sleep and…no Brad.

Her breath caught. Where had that come from?

"Abby, darlin', are you all right?" Brad asked, interrupting her disturbing thoughts.

Glancing over at him, she nodded. "Of course. Why do you ask?"

"You seem like you're a million miles away," he said, smiling. "You aren't about to concede our wager are you?"

She laughed. "Not on your life."

"I asked if you thought it was about time for us to get the twins changed into their pajamas and give them their snack," he said, smiling. He nodded at the yawning little girls at his sides. "Any more of watching the singing teapot and the French candelabra and these two are going to be out like a couple of lights."

"Do you want me to get them ready or can you handle it?" she asked.

Abby smiled when she realized they were both avoiding mentioning the words *sleep* or *bed*. Having seen Sadie get the girls ready for bed before, she had firsthand knowledge of the fuss they raised when key words were mentioned.

Brad shrugged. "It doesn't matter to me who gets them changed. Is Sunnie asleep?"

Nodding, Abby rose to her feet. "I'll take her upstairs

and put her in her crib. When I come back down, I'll get Wendy and Gail into their pajamas while you get the snacks Sadie left for them."

He stretched his arms along the back of the couch. "Sounds like we have a plan."

"You sound a little tired," she said, grinning.

"Just wait and see, darlin'," he said, laughing. "I'm going to come out the winner on that bet."

"Hang on to that little dream, Mr. Price," she said, walking down the hall.

Twenty minutes later, the twins had been dressed in their matching pink-footed pajamas and were just finishing their cheese flavored crackers shaped like goldfish and their milk when the doorbell rang.

"I didn't expect them back this soon," Abby said, picking up a handful of plastic blocks to place into a mesh bag.

"Sadie told me they were only going out for dinner." Brad chuckled. "I think they wanted to enjoy a meal for a change without a toddler food fight."

"Just think, you have that to look forward to with Sunnie," Abby said, grinning.

"And here I thought those days were over when I graduated college." He started down the hall to open the door. "I'll have to give Zeke and Chris a call to come over and join the fun. They used to like a good food fight."

"Unless you want your housekeeper to quit, I wouldn't if I were you," she advised.

A half hour later, after bidding good-night to Sadie, Rick and the twins, Abby found herself alone with Brad for the first time since the humiliating incident the night before. Fortunately, he hadn't brought up the subject and she was grateful for that. But it was time to discuss another uncomfortable matter.

"There's something we need to talk over," she said, making sure she wasn't standing under the mistletoe. Knowing his newfound fondness for the holiday tradition, he would probably insist on kissing her again, and she needed her wits about her.

He stared at her for several seconds as if trying to determine what she wanted to tell him. "If it's about what happened when I kissed you—"

"It's not," she interrupted. "Well, not exactly."

"Okay," he said, placing his hand to her back to guide her toward the kitchen. "I'll make us some coffee."

Shaking her head, she stopped in the middle of the foyer. "Thank you, but I won't be here that long." She took a deep breath. "I won't be going with you to the Christmas Ball."

His frown was filled with displeasure. "Why not?"

"There's been some talk among several of the TCC members about our spending so much time together," she stated flatly. "I don't like it and I want it to stop. Our attending the ball together will only increase the gossip, not put a halt to it."

"I don't give a damn what people say and you shouldn't, either." A muscle worked along his lean jaw, and she could tell that Brad wasn't in the least bit happy. "First of all, it's none of their business. And second, if we don't go together now, the rumors will only increase."

"How do you figure that?" she asked. Sometimes his logic was hard to follow.

"Think about it. If there's talk about our seeing each other and we aren't together, then they'll start speculating about that," he explained. He cupped her face with his hands. "Don't you see, Abby? No matter what we do, people are going to talk. We can't control that."

"Unfortunately," she said, feeling trapped.

"But there is a way for us to take charge of the situation." He held her questioning gaze with his. "We don't have anything to hide. We can go together with our heads held high and show them that we don't care what's said, that we'll do whatever we damned well please."

She supposed it made sense when put that way. By ignoring the gossipmongers, she and Brad took the power away from them. But that wasn't going to keep her from feeling uncomfortable with the entire situation.

She nodded. "I suppose you're right."

"I know I am, darlin'."

He lowered his head to fuse his lips with hers and just as she feared, her will to resist was nonexistent. She had told herself she wouldn't allow him to kiss her, wouldn't take the chance on making a fool of herself again. But the truth of the matter was, she wanted his kiss, wanted to feel his body pressed close to hers, and whether it was wise or not, she wanted him.

That fact alone should have been enough to send her running as far and fast as her legs could carry her. Instead, she raised her arms to his shoulders and threaded her fingers in the hair at the nape of his neck as she surrendered herself to the mind-altering feelings she had come to expect from his kiss.

When he slipped his hand beneath her blouse, the feel of his large, warm palm caressing her waist, then sliding up along her ribs, caused a delicious warmth to flow through her from the top of her head all the way to her toes. But when he deepened the kiss at the same time his hand covered her breast, the heat within her settled low in the pit of her stomach and caused her knees to give way. Sagging against him, she felt the evidence of his desire and an answering ache formed in the most feminine part of her.

His thumb teasing her through the fabric of her bra, and the ridge of his hard arousal pressed to her lower belly quickly had her aching for him to touch her without the encumbrance of their clothing. She wanted to feel his hard flesh against her much softer skin, needed to touch and explore his body as she wanted him to explore hers.

Lost in the passionate sensations Brad had created, she whimpered when he eased away from the kiss and removed his hand from beneath her shirt. Resting his forehead against hers, he took a deep breath, then another.

"I know I'm going to regret this, but I think it's time for you to go home and get a good night's sleep," he said, his voice hoarse as he released her to get her coat from the closet. "You look as tired as I feel."

She slipped her arms into the jacket he held for her, and a bit of the tension that still gripped her began to ease as she realized what he had said a few moments earlier. Walking to the door, she turned back to smile at him. "You're tired?"

Frowning, he nodded. "Aren't you?"

"A little," she said, stepping out onto the porch. Turning back, she added, "But you mentioned it first, Mr. Price. Now you owe me dinner."

Smiling as he watched the door close behind Abby, Brad stuffed his hands in the front pockets of his jeans and rocked back on his heels. He hadn't forgotten about the wager. He had made it a point to see that she won. It had been well worth conceding just to see the triumphant look on her pretty face.

But as he stood there thinking about how special he intended to make the evening for her when he paid up on the bet, the thought of her being upset over the gossip among some of the TCC members began to burn at his gut. He had a feeling that the majority of those talking behind their backs were from the faction that clung to tradition—those who had wanted to keep the prestigious club an all-male organization and resented that Abby had joined the ranks.

He drew in a deep breath. It wasn't something he was overly proud of, but until recently he had been in complete agreement with them. But now?

Times had changed, and in order to make sure the club remained relevant and an institution of high regard in the Royal community, the membership had to be more progressive in their thinking. Abby had been a member for most of the past year, and he could honestly say that in that length of time nothing had changed about the club's mission. The entire membership, including Abby devoted themselves to upholding the values set forth by Tex Langley over a hundred years ago.

That's why the gossip had to stop. Besides the fact that it was upsetting Abby, if it kept up, the club would end up destroying itself from within. The honor they had all pledged to uphold was already in jeopardy. Fortunately, he was pretty sure he had a way to put a stop to all the backbiting, and that was exactly what he intended to do.

The next afternoon, Brad sat at the head of the heavy mahogany conference table in one of the private meeting rooms in the TCC clubhouse, waiting to brief his two friends on his plan. Provided for members to strategize the various secret missions of goodwill they had carried out over the years, the meeting rooms were available to any member with an objective to right a wrong.

"What's up, Brad?" Chris asked as he and Zeke entered the room.

"Some of the members have been pretty vocal about the time I've been spending with Abby Langley and I intend to put a stop to it," he said bluntly.

Zeke nodded as he pulled out the chair to one side of Brad and sat down. "I overheard a couple of them gossiping about it the other day at the diner, but as soon as I walked by, they had the good sense to shut up."

Brad didn't ask what was said. He didn't care to know. That he and Abby were the topic of conversation was enough to upset Abby, and that, in turn, didn't set well with him.

"Yeah, my father-in-law mentioned that the two of

you were getting pretty tight," Chris said, taking the seat on the other side of Brad. "Harrison asked if I knew anything about it, and I told him I wouldn't discuss it with him if I did."

"Thanks." Brad appreciated his friends' loyalty. "I have an idea how to pretty much put a stop to it, but I'm going to need your help."

"You know you can count us in," Zeke said emphatically.

"You bet," Chris agreed. "What did you have in mind?"

"I'd like to get the word out that Abby and I are working on restoring unity to the club," Brad said.

Chris nodded. "That sounds reasonable. No matter which of you wins the presidency, the members backing the loser are going to have their nose out of joint."

"Do you have a plan on how to go about letting people know?" Zeke asked.

"If the two of you could mention it to a few of the biggest windbags in the club, I think the word would spread pretty quick," Brad explained. "By the time the election results are announced at the Christmas Ball, the members will hopefully be thinking along the lines of maintaining the club's integrity and make the transition easier for whichever one of us is elected."

"Sounds like a solid plan to me," Chris said.

Zeke grinned. "Nothing against Abby, but this is the very reason you need to win the office. If there's a chance in hell to get the TCC back on track, you're it."

A look of anticipation crossed Chris's face. "I'll tell Harrison Reynolds. It'll be all over town by the end of the day. It's my bet he's one of the windbags that's been speculating on what's going on."

"You're calling your father-in-law a windbag? I thought you and he had buried the hatchet and called a truce," Brad said, referring to the animosity the older man had displayed for Chris in years past. A self-made man, Chris came from a modest background and his father-in-law had never thought Chris was good enough for his daughter, Macy.

"We have made peace," Chris admitted. "But only to a point. He still forgets himself from time to time and gets in his digs about me being born on the other side of the tracks."

Zeke uttered a graphic curse that had them all nodding their heads. "He'd be lucky if he was half the man you are, Chris."

Chris shrugged. "We'll never be best friends, that's for damned sure. But we both love Macy, and we've worked out our differences enough to tolerate each other for her sake."

"Anything else?" Zeke asked.

"I got a call from Mitch Hayward this morning, asking for a few more details about managing the football team," Brad said, grinning. "It looks like he's about to commit."

"Man, that's awesome," Zeke said, grinning.

"Do you think he'll make his decision before the Christmas Ball?" Chris asked, sounding hopeful.

"It looks like he might," Brad said. "It would be nice to make the announcements about the team at the Ball. By that time, we should have commitments from a couple of Mitch's former pro teammates for the other management positions we'll have open."

Checking his watch, Zeke rose to his feet. "There should be several of the TCC members at the diner right now having coffee. I think I'll drop in and set your plan into motion. The sooner we get the word out, the better."

"And I'll stop by Reynolds Construction to set things straight on that front," Chris assured, standing to leave.

As Brad followed his best friends out of the club-house, he felt confident that by evening there wouldn't be any more speculation about why he and Abby had been spending so much time together. Or if there was, it would have a more positive spin.

Seven

In the few days that followed their babysitting Sadie and Rick's twins, Abby hadn't seen Brad and Sunnie at all, and she had spoken to Brad on the phone only a few times. She had been busy with the party she volunteered to help with for the children at the women's shelter, as well as getting up in the wee hours of the morning several days in a row to place the pink flamingos on the lawns of the unsuspecting wealthier residents of Royal.

As she parked the SUV in front of his house, her heart sped up in anticipation. She took pride in the fact that hers and others' efforts had raised several hundred thousand dollars in donations for the worthwhile charity. But as fulfilling as it was to be of service to the community, she had missed seeing Sunnie and her devastatingly handsome uncle. It wasn't wise and would probably end up causing her immense emotional upset, but she hadn't been able to stop it. Brad and his precious niece were becoming an extremely important part of her life.

Before she could knock, Brad swung the door open and pulled her into his arms. "Are you ready for the culinary event of the year?" he asked, giving her a kiss that made her head spin.

"I—I…suppose so," she said, feeling delightfully breathless.

"Good." He took her by the hand. "Close your eyes."

"What are you up to this time?" she asked, laughing.

His smile caused her pulse to flutter. "Our bet was for the loser to make a nice dinner for the winner. Now, close your eyes."

When she did as he commanded, he led her through the house to the formal dining room. "Okay, you can open them now," he whispered close to her ear.

She opened her eyes and looked at the table. "Oh, my! Brad, this is gorgeous!"

The red place mats and green napkins contrasted beautifully with the pristine white tablecloth. An elegant silver vase filled with at least two dozen dark red roses served as a centerpiece, with silver candlesticks holding lit red tapers standing on either side.

She hadn't expected him to go to such lengths. Thinking he would prepare something simple for dinner like spaghetti, possibly served at the kitchen table, she was touched by the thought and effort he had obviously put into the meal.

Standing behind her, he wrapped his arms around

her waist to pull her back against him. "Only the best for you, darlin'."

His warm breath on the side of her neck and the feel of him pressed against her back side sent tiny electric charges streaking through every part of her. She might have fought what was happening between them at first, but over the course of the past couple of weeks, he had worn her down and she had come to look forward to their time together, to his gestures of affection. It seemed that Brad used every excuse imaginable to touch her cheek or her hair, or kiss her until they both gasped for breath. And God help her, she loved every single minute of it.

She realized she was playing a dangerous game and that frightened her. But as long as she kept things in perspective and didn't allow herself to start caring too much, she should be able to maintain their newfound friendship and still protect herself from being hurt.

In theory it all sounded good, but putting it into practice might prove difficult. With Brad holding her, nibbling tiny kisses along the column of her neck, it was becoming harder to remember why it was so important to keep from giving him her heart.

"Where's the baby?" she asked, trying to distract herself from her disturbing thoughts.

"She's spending the night with Sadie and Rick," he whispered against her skin. "I thought it would be nice for you and I to have an evening to ourselves for a change."

The idea of spending the entire evening alone with Brad, without the buffer of having to take care of the baby, should have sent her running for the door. That it didn't bothered her even more.

"Are you sure that's...wise?" she asked. It was more a question for herself than it was for him.

He turned her to face him, then cupping her face with his hands, met her questioning gaze. "I give you my word that nothing is going to happen unless you want it to, darlin'."

She wasn't about to tell him that was what worried her. She didn't have to. They both knew that the chemistry between them was stronger than either had ever imagined was possible.

"Why don't we have the wonderful dinner you promised me?" she asked, avoiding the subject of what might happen later.

Brad stared at her a moment longer, then smiling, pulled out one of the dining room chairs. "Let's get you seated for the best Bourbon Street steak you've ever had."

She wasn't surprised they were having steak. Most Texas men preferred a good steak to any other kind of meal.

"Which restaurant did the catering?" she asked when he brought two plates in from the kitchen.

"Chez Price," he said, setting her plate down in front of her.

"You did the marinade, as well as grilled the steaks?" she asked.

"Why are you so surprised?" he asked, sitting down at the head of the table. "The bet was that the loser had to make dinner."

"I know, but most men I know think that throwing

steaks on the grill is good enough," she said, placing her napkin in her lap. "They don't even consider marinating them."

He gave her a teasing smile as he reached for his knife and fork. "Darlin', haven't you figured out by now that I'm not like most men?"

As she took a bite of the succulent-looking steak, Abby had to admit that over the past couple of months, Brad had been full of surprises. First he had stepped forward to take on the responsibility of raising his brother's child as his own. That was completely out of character for a self-confessed playboy. Then, when he told her that he had taken a leave of absence from his financial planning firm to stay home with Sunnie because he didn't think it would be in her best interest to turn her over to a nanny, she had really been taken aback. Abby knew for a fact that was unheard of among men of his caliber in the business world. But the biggest surprise of all had come the night that Sunnie had the reaction to the immunization shot. Brad had not only been extremely worried about the baby, he had extended that concern to her as well when, knowing how tired she was, he had refused to wake her for the drive home.

"How do you like your steak?" he asked, interrupting her introspection.

"It's delicious," she said, meaning it.

"Good." He picked up his glass of iced tea. "Do they have any good steak houses in Seattle?"

Smiling, she nodded. "There's a place in Redmond called the Stone House that has excellent steaks."

"Is that the suburb where you lived when you were out there?"

"No, Redmond was where my partners and I started our software company." She smiled fondly as she thought of the billion-dollar business they had built from the ground up. "We used to eat dinner there when we had to work late."

"I've heard your computer program is the gold standard for the insurance industry." He set his glass back on the table. "Do you think you'll ever go back to work in software development?"

"I gave it some thought right after Richard died, and my former partners have recently approached me about starting a new company," she admitted. "But I would have to move back to the Seattle area and I'm not sure I want to do that. I have the ranch to take care of and…" Pausing, she grinned. "…when I win the TCC presidency, I think the membership would prefer that I live a little closer to Royal."

Brad laughed as he rose to take their plates into the kitchen. "You're pretty sure of yourself there, aren't you, Langley?"

"No more so than you are," she said, enjoying their good-natured banter.

When he returned to the dining room, he held out his hand. "I thought we would have dessert in front of the fireplace."

"That sounds nice," she said, placing her hand in his.

Rising from the chair, she let him lead her into the family room where he had set a silver tray with two champagne flutes and a bowl of chocolate-dipped strawberries on the coffee table. A bucket of ice sat to the side chilling a bottle of champagne. The fireplace and the twinkling lights from the Christmas tree in the corner were the only illumination in the otherwise dark room.

Before she could comment on the scene obviously set for seduction, Brad put his arms around her. "I want you to know that I'm not planning anything but a nice relaxing evening. Anything that progresses beyond that is going to be your call, darlin'."

Abby appreciated his candidness, as well as his willingness to give her control of the situation. But considering the way she melted into a wanton puddle of need whenever he kissed her, she wasn't certain that leaving how the evening would go up to her was the best of ideas.

"I didn't think you drank anything alcoholic," she said, deciding not to address the subject until she had to.

"I normally don't," he said, slowly rubbing his cheek against her hair. "But I made an exception for tonight."

"W-why?" she asked, distracted by his warm breath whispering over her skin and the feel of his muscular frame pressed against her much softer one.

"There's something we need to do," he said, releasing her to remove the bottle from the ice bucket. He popped the cork and poured the sparkling pink liquid into the flutes. "One of us is going to become the new president of the Texas Cattleman's Club tomorrow evening, and as soon as the announcement is made, whoever wins will be asked to give a little speech. After that we'll be surrounded by members congratulating whoever wins." He handed her one of the glasses. "I'd rather have a quiet moment to celebrate with you, and tonight is about the only time that's going to happen."

His thoughtfulness touched her. Raising her glass, she lightly touched his. "Congratulations to whoever wins."

"To us," he said, taking a sip of the champagne. He reached down to pick up one of the strawberries, then held it to her lips. "In the event that you win, I can't think of anyone I'd rather lose to, Abby."

"Nor I, you," she said, taking a bite of the strawberry.

Her breath caught when he leaned forward to kiss away a drop of the berry juice from her lips. "You taste good."

"Champagne and chocolate-covered strawberries always taste good together," she agreed.

His smoldering gaze made her heart flutter wildly. "I wasn't talking about the berries or the champagne, darlin'."

When he took their flutes to set them on the coffee table, the look in his eyes reflected his intent, and she automatically swayed toward him as he wrapped his arms around her.

The moment his mouth covered hers, Abby knew the decision had been made. She wanted Brad's kiss, wanted to feel his body tight with desire, wanted to taste his passion. And heaven help her, she wanted him to experience the same things from her as well.

Pulling Abby to him, Brad savored the taste of champagne, strawberries and chocolate on her perfect coral lips. He didn't think he had ever tasted anything as erotic or as sensual in all of his thirty-two years.

But when he deepened the kiss to tease and coax, her passion, the desire he detected in her eager response, was everything he had hoped for and more. In the beginning, she might have fought against the attraction that drew them together, but he knew as sure as the sun came up in the mornings that Abby had been as powerless to resist it as he had been.

When she wrapped her arms around his waist and took the initiative to excite him as he had been doing to her, his heart thumped against his ribs like a jackhammer, and it felt as if every drop of blood in his body rushed to the area south of his belt buckle. His arousal was almost instantaneous and made him feel slightly dizzy from its intensity.

Without so much as a second thought, he slid his hands down her back to her shapely bottom and drew her forward to rest more fully against him. He wanted her to feel what she did to him, how much she made him want her.

He felt a shiver course through her a moment before she tightened her arms around him, and he could tell she was as turned on as he was. "You're driving me crazy, darlin'," he said, his voice sounding rusty.

"I think...it's mutual." She sounded as winded as he felt.

Bringing his hand up to thread his fingers through her long wavy hair, he leaned back to look into her vibrant blue eyes. "I'm not going to lie to you, Abby. I want you more than I want my next breath. But I swear I didn't intentionally set out to seduce you this evening.

If you would rather we sit down and just talk, I'm okay with that." He knew he would suffer something awful if she chose the latter, but he could live with that as long as she was comfortable with whatever decision she made.

She sent his blood pressure soaring when she put her index finger to his lips and shook her head. "I don't have the will to fight this any longer and I don't want to talk. I want you, Brad."

"Are you sure?" he found himself asking. If she changed her mind, he had a feeling he would go stark raving mad. But he wasn't going to push for more if she wasn't ready to take things to the next level.

"There are a lot of things I'm not sure of, but this isn't one of them, Brad," she said seriously. "Yes, I want you."

Cradling her face with his palms, he gazed down at her. "Once we go upstairs to my bedroom, there won't be any turning back, darlin'. We'll cross a line and things will never be the same between us again."

"I know."

"And I don't want there to be any regrets," he added.

She closed her eyes a moment, then opening them, stared up at him. "The only possibility of my regretting anything is if we don't make love," she said softly.

The strength in her tone and the truth in her expressive eyes were all the answer he needed. Stepping away from her, he walked over to switch off the gas log in the fireplace, then turn the lights off on the Christmas tree.

Neither spoke when he returned to take her hand in his and lead her down the hall to climb the stairs.

Words were unnecessary. They both knew the risk they were taking and that they could never go back to the way things had been between them.

Walking into the master suite, he closed the door behind them. He switched on the lamp in the sitting room and turned to take her into his arms. He had every intention of going slow, of savoring every second of his first night making love to her. That there would be many more nights wasn't in question. He wasn't sure how he knew that. He just did. And he never doubted his instincts.

He kissed her slowly, thoroughly, then, raising his head to capture her gaze with his, he slowly tugged her teal blouse from the waistband of her black slacks. "You don't know how many times in the past couple of weeks I've thought about doing this," he said, as he reached up to release the small pearl button at the top of the garment.

"Probably as many times as I've thought about this," she said, unbuttoning the top of his shirt. Her fingertips brushed the skin along his collarbone and sent fire streaking through his veins.

By the time they released the last buttons on her blouse and his shirt, Brad felt as if he had run a race. As he slid his hands beneath each side of the silk fabric and along her ribs, Abby pressed her palms against his chest. He could have sworn that he had been branded.

"I've also wanted to do this since seeing you without your shirt the other night," she said, tracing the ridges of his abdomen and testing the strength of his pectoral muscles.

Feeling as if the air had been sucked from the room,

he struggled to draw in some much-needed oxygen. "Why don't we get this out of the way?" he asked, sliding the teal silk over her slender shoulders and down her arms.

When he tossed her blouse to the side, he closed his eyes and enjoyed the feel of her hands skimming across his shoulders as she pushed his shirt off as well. "I never realized how beautiful your body is," she said, tracing her finger down the thin line of hair below his navel.

He sucked in a sharp breath and forced himself to stand still as her finger followed it to the waistband of his dress trousers. "I wouldn't say my body…is all that great." He concentrated on what she had said in an effort to slow down the flood of desire pumping through his veins. Running his finger along the lace edge of her bra, he released the front clasp on the scrap of lace and silk with a flick of his fingers. "I'm all hard angles and ridges," he said, sliding it from her body to toss it on top of her blouse and his shirt lying on the carpet beside them. "You're the one with the perfect body," he said, cupping her with his hands. "You're soft, curvy and…" He lowered his head to kiss the puckered tip of each full breast. "…so sweet."

Rewarded by her soft moan, he wrapped his arms around her to pull her to him. He groaned at the contact of his hair-roughened flesh meeting her softer, feminine skin. "You feel good, darlin'."

"So…do you." Her sigh of contentment feathering over his bare chest sent a shaft of heat straight to his groin.

Wanting to feel all of her against him, he took a

step back, then after kneeling to remove their shoes, he straightened and reached for the button and zipper at her waist. "Look at me, Abby," he commanded, as he slid his fingers beneath the waistband of her slacks and panties. When the black linen and silk fell to the floor, she stepped out of them, then used her foot to push them toward the growing pile of their clothes.

"You're breathtaking, Abby," he said, forcing himself to breathe as he drank in the sight of her. Beautiful in every way, her confidence and pride sent his pulse racing, and the only word he could think to describe the moment was *perfection*.

"Don't you think you're a little overdressed for the occasion?" she asked, her velvet voice sending a shaft of heat right through him.

"That can be remedied right now," he said, making short work of removing his tailored slacks and boxer briefs.

Tossing them on the pile at their feet, he didn't immediately step forward and pull her to him. He was determined not to rush. He was going to make the night the most magical experience of both their lives or die trying. But it was damned difficult, considering the most exciting woman he had ever known stood before him, caressing every inch of his body with her eyes. She wanted him as badly as he wanted her, and the knowledge that she would soon be his robbed him of breath.

Without a word, he held out his arms, and to his immense satisfaction she stepped forward to melt against him. Their bodies touching from shoulders to knees fanned the flames building in his lower body and made his knees feel as if they were about to buckle.

He leaned back, and their gazes met. Without a word, he swung her up into his arms and carried her into the bedroom. He paused at the side of the bed long enough for Abby to pull the comforter and sheet back, then gently lowered her to the mattress.

Giving him a smile that lit the darkest corners of his soul, Abby raised her arms in invitation. "Make love to me, Brad."

His heart hammered inside his chest as he stretched out beside her and took her back into his arms. "I want to take this slow," he said, clenching his teeth against the wave of need coursing through him. "But I'm not sure that's going to be possible, darlin'."

She shook her head. "I don't think so, either. It's been so long."

He kissed the fluttering pulse at the base of her throat at the same time he ran his hand from her back, along her side and up to cover her full breast. "There's been no one since—"

"No," she whispered, cutting him off his question as if not wanting to mention her late husband's name.

Brad could respect that. He didn't particularly want her reminded of the man. Richard Langley would always be a part of her past. There was no getting around that. But he wanted her to think of Brad Price as her future.

The thought should have scared the hell out of him. It didn't. Deciding there would be plenty of time later to figure out why it didn't, he lowered his head and fused their lips.

He reacquainted himself with her sweetness at the same time he moved his hand back down her side to the curve of her hip, then down her leg. Her flawless skin beneath his palm felt like satin and he didn't think he could ever get enough of touching her. When she restlessly moved her legs, he knew the sensations within her were building. Easing his hand down to her inner thigh, he stopped just short of his goal.

"Do you want me to bring you pleasure, Abby?"

"Y-yes."

Nibbling tiny kisses along her collarbone, he parted her to tease and stroke, to make sure she was ready for him. Her tiny moan of need, the fact that she wanted him as badly as he wanted her, sent fire streaking through his veins. But when she moved her hand from his chest down his abdomen to do a little exploring of her own, Brad felt as if his head might fly right off his shoulders.

"Darlin', I love the way your hands feel on my body," he said, capturing her hand with his. "But if you keep that up, you're going to be disappointed and I'm going to be mighty embarrassed."

"I want you, Brad."

"Now?"

"Y-yes!"

The level of desire he detected in her voice was all the encouragement he needed, and parting her legs with his knee, he eased himself over her. His heart stalled when she reached down to guide him to her, and he had to struggle to hold onto what little control he had left.

Slowly, carefully, he pushed his hips forward, and he felt her body accept him with an eagerness that threatened to rob him of every good intention he had of taking things slow. He clenched his teeth and fought the need to thrust into her. It had been over a year since Abby had made love, and she needed time to adjust.

As he watched for any trace of discomfort, she closed her eyes and a slight smile curved her lips. "You feel wonderful," she said, wrapping her arms around his shoulders.

Gathering her close, he sank himself deep inside of her and, holding himself perfectly still, covered her mouth with his. He wanted to draw out the pleasure, to make it last as long as possible. But his need for her was greater than anything he could have imagined, and apparently she felt the same way about him. When she wrapped her legs around him and arched her back, he sank even deeper and there was no way he could stop himself from rocking against her.

The combination of his need for her and her ready acceptance of his body joining with hers was mind-blowing and quickly had the pleasure spiraling out of control. He felt her tighten around him and knew she was close to reaching the pinnacle they both sought.

Several moments later, he heard her soft gasp as the building pressure overtook her. Tiny feminine muscles caressed him and quickly had him joining her as together they got caught up in the spiraling sensations of their release.

As they slowly drifted back to reality, Brad held Abby close. What they had just shared was more powerful, more meaningful, than he could have ever imagined.

"Are you all right?" he asked, raising his head from her shoulder.

Nodding, she smiled. "That was amazing."

"You're amazing," he said, kissing the tip of her nose. He eased to her side and pulled her to him. "Spend the night with me."

"I'm not sure that's—"

He placed his finger to her lips. He knew it had to be difficult for her to cast aside years of caring what others thought of her, but it was time she realized people were going to talk no matter what choices she made.

"I don't give a damn what anyone thinks and you shouldn't either, Abby. We're adults." He gave her a smile to soften his words. "We don't need permission or approval to spend time together."

"I know you're right," she said slowly.

He gave her a wicked grin as he moved his hips to press himself against her. "Now, let's concentrate more on what I'm thinking and less about what anyone else thinks."

Eight

As Abby put the finishing touches on her makeup, she looked at the woman in the mirror staring back at her. Less than twenty-four hours ago, she had stood in front of the same mirror, getting ready to go to Brad's for a nice dinner, some stimulating conversation and, as she had come to expect from him, a couple of steamy kisses. Nothing more. But instead of leaving at the end of the evening as she had planned on doing, all he had to do was kiss her and she had ended up spending the entire night with him.

She sighed as she walked into her bedroom to take off her robe and pick up the long, black evening gown she had laid out on the bed before her shower. After they had made love for the second time, he had teased and cajoled her into doing as he asked, and that was what she couldn't understand. No one had ever been able to talk her into doing something she didn't want to do. Yet Brad seemed to be able to talk her into doing whatever he wanted.

Closing her eyes for a moment, Abby took a deep breath and shook her head. She had to stop lying to herself. No matter how unwise, no matter how complicated it made things for her, the truth was she hadn't wanted to leave. She had wanted every one of his kisses, wanted to experience the degree of passion that he created within her and wanted him to make love to her.

When she stepped into the dress, the clingy fabric sliding over her skin reminded her of the way Brad's hands had felt as he explored and teased to heighten the exquisite pleasure that had all but consumed her. A shiver of longing streaked up her spine—just the thought of their lovemaking left her breathless.

As she stepped into her black high heels and walked over to get her earrings from the jewelry box, she wished she could tell herself that what she had shared with Brad was nothing more than two lonely people coming together for the physical intimacy missing in their lives. But in all honesty, she couldn't.

Glancing at the rings Richard had given her on their wedding day, which were tucked into one corner of the jewelry chest, Abby knew that her lovemaking with Brad had been far more than just the need to once again be desired by a man. And that confused her more than anything else.

She had loved her late husband for as long as she could remember. They had been together since her freshman year in high school, but in all those years, both before and after they were married, the passion and desire in their relationship had never been as intense as what she had shared with Brad. What she had with Richard had been more sedate, more... comfortable.

Abby frowned. "What an odd way to describe a marriage," she said aloud. Surely she and Richard had more going for them than...

The sound of the doorbell interrupted her disturbing thoughts and, quickly fastening her earrings, she picked up her sequined clutch and left the bedroom. She fully intended to give the state of her marriage more thought, but it would have to wait until later when she was alone and not getting ready to go out for the evening.

On her way down the hall to answer the door, she couldn't help but notice that her pulse sped up and her step was a bit quicker than usual from the anticipation of seeing Brad again. That gave her a bit of an uneasy feeling, but she didn't have time to dwell on it as she opened the front door.

The look in Brad's eyes when he saw her caused her heart to skip a beat. Without a word he stepped forward to wrap her in his arms. He gave her a kiss that left her breathless, then stepped back to look at her again.

"You're absolutely breathtaking, Abby."

"I could say the same about you," she said honestly. Dressed in a black tuxedo, white pleated shirt and black bow tie, he could have easily been a cover model for *GQ*.

Opening a small florist's box that she hadn't noticed before, he removed a beautiful white orchid. "Let's get this pinned into place before we leave."

His fingers brushed her breast as he positioned the

delicate corsage, sending excitement skipping over every nerve in her body. "Thank you, Brad. It's beautiful."

He shook his head as he worked the pin through the fabric of her evening gown. "It pales in comparison to you, darlin'." He smiled. "Are you ready for the biggest night of the year in Royal, Texas?"

"As ready as I'll ever be," she said, nodding as he helped her with her shawl. As he guided her down the porch steps and out to the waiting limo, she asked, "Who's watching Sunnie for the evening?"

"Juanita got back from Dallas after you left this morning and agreed to watch the baby and the twins for the evening." Helping her into the back seat, he chuckled. "This time last year, I never dreamed that I'd be arranging for a babysitter and leaving phone numbers where I could be reached in case of an emergency."

"Having a baby in the house changes everything," Abby said, wishing she had a baby to give her life meaning.

As the chauffeur drove them to the Christmas Ball, neither mentioned that in just a few short hours one of them would become the new president of the Texas Cattleman's Club, while the other would go home the loser.

"Do you know how much I missed you after you left this morning?" he asked, his voice taking on a low, intimate tone.

"I...uh, no," she said, feeling as if the temperature in the car rose several degrees.

"All I could think about was how good you felt last

night and how much I wanted you again," he said, his hazel eyes darkening with desire.

Thankful the window between the driver and the backseat was closed, Abby smiled. "Last night was wonderful."

The smoldering look he gave her curled her toes. "I give you my word, darlin', tonight's going to be even better."

Just the thought of spending another night in Brad's arms caused her already fluttering pulse to race. "But Sunnie—"

"—will be sound asleep," he said, as the driver steered the car up the drive to the TCC clubhouse.

Before she could respond, the chauffeur opened the back door of the limo and Brad got out of the car, then turned to help her to her feet. "We'll have to talk about that later," she warned, as they passed the uniformed doorman.

"I'll look forward to it," Brad said, his tone suggestive.

Two or three times a year the normally relaxed atmosphere of the clubhouse was transformed into formal social events, with the Christmas Ball being the biggest and most elaborate. Already decorated for Christmas, a canopy of white twinkle lights had been added to give the entrance to the establishment a magical feel.

Abby marveled at the staff's obvious hard work. "This is stunning," she said, looking around at the multitude of potted poinsettias and hanging pine boughs. "I've never seen it look quite like this."

"I know you said you didn't attend last year, but

haven't you been here for the Ball before?" Brad asked, as they walked toward the ballroom.

Abby, nodded. "It's been years, and I really don't remember the old building looking quite this charming."

"That's why it will be a shame if the vote goes in favor of the new building," he said, shaking his head. "I'm all for progress, but there has to be a way to preserve this tradition and still move forward."

It hadn't been a secret that Brad had been among the ranks of members in favor of keeping the old clubhouse instead of building a new one. "Has Sadie talked to you about what she would like to do with the clubhouse if the members vote for a new building?" Abby asked.

He looked puzzled. "No. Does she have something in mind?"

Looking up, Abby noticed Sadie and Rick Pruitt walking toward them. "Why don't you ask her yourself? I'm sure she could explain her ideas much better than I could.

"Sadie, you look gorgeous." Abby hugged her friend. "I love your dress."

Brad's sister smiled. "And I love yours. Rick and I were just commenting on what a nice couple the two of you make when you got out of the limo."

Before Abby could correct Sadie and tell her that they were just attending the ball together, Brad asked, "So I hear you have plans for the old clubhouse?"

Sadie glanced at Abby, who nodded. "I was telling him that you might be interested in the building."

While Sadie outlined her ideas for turning the clubhouse into a family cultural center, Zeke and Sheila Travers joined them. "Are you ready to become the first female president of the Texas Cattleman's Club?" Sheila whispered.

Abby smiled. "I haven't been elected yet, but yes, I think I'm up for the challenge." Concerned that the last time she had seen Sheila, the woman hadn't been feeling well, Abby asked, "You must be over the flu. You're positively glowing tonight."

Zeke's grin could have lit a small town. "There's a reason for that." Leaning down to kiss his wife's cheek, he asked, "Would you like to tell them or should I?"

"You go ahead," Sheila said, gazing lovingly at her husband.

"It turns out that Sheila hasn't had the flu for the past couple of weeks after all." Zeke put his arm around his wife's shoulders and hugged her to his side. "We just found out we're pregnant."

"I'm so happy for you," Abby said, hugging the beautiful mocha-skinned woman.

Sheila was one of the kindest, sweetest women Abby had ever known, and she knew how much Sheila had wanted a child. It was something they had both had in common. Now it looked as if Sheila's hopes had come true, and Abby was truly happy for her. She only wished that by some miracle, hers would, too.

"Are you okay?" Brad whispered close to her ear, as he put his arm around her.

"O-of course," she said, touched by his consideration. He knew how much she wanted a baby, and he must have sensed how heart-wrenching it was to see others realize their dreams, all the while knowing that she never would.

"Honey, I think Summer Franklin is trying to get

your attention," Rick said, motioning toward a gathering of other members and their wives standing across the way. Zeke's business partner, Darius Franklin, stood at its center.

"I'll be right back," Sadie said, hurrying over to see what the coordinator of the Helping Hands Women's Shelter needed.

While they waited for Sadie to return to the group, Mitch Taylor and his wife, Jennifer, walked over to say hello. "Are you two ready for the big announcement?" Mitch asked. He was the interim president of the TCC, and Abby thought he looked extremely happy to be stepping down and letting someone else take over the job.

"I've been looking forward to this for months," Brad said happily.

"Abby, how many more days will the flamingos be showing up in people's yards?" Jennifer asked, laughing. "I thought our neighbor, Mr. Hargraves, was going to suffer a stroke the other morning when he got up to find them on his lawn."

The man in question was legendary for his thrifty ways, and it must have come as quite a shock to think that he was actually going to have to part with some of his money to get rid of the plastic birds. "I think New Year's Eve is scheduled to be the end of this year's campaign," Abby said, laughing with the woman. "Apparently, Mr. Hargraves made a donation to get rid of them, because I saw them on someone else's lawn this morning."

Abby noticed Brad and Mitch exchange a look. "Is something going on?" she asked.

Brad shook his head, as Mitch and Jennifer walked away to mingle with some of the other attendees. "We've been working on a little project together, and we intend to make an announcement about it sometime during the evening."

She had a good idea she knew what they were going to tell everyone. During the campaign he had taken great pains to let it be known that he was thinking about buying a semipro football team and moving it to Royal. Some had thought it was a ploy to gain more votes for the presidency, since he had waited to tell everyone after the campaigning was in full swing. Apparently that hadn't been the case, although she suspected that it hadn't hurt his run for office.

"You bought the football team?" she guessed.

Placing his index finger to her lips, he nodded. "Zeke, Chris and I are co-owners, and Mitch has agreed to be the general manager," he said close to her ear. "But we want to wait to tell everyone until after the new officers are announced."

"That's wonderful. The town has needed something like this for a long time," she said, meaning it.

For the majority of the townspeople, Houston and Dallas were too far away to attend a professional football game more than once or twice during the season. Having a semiprofessional team in town would allow them to enjoy going to games more often.

"Well, the list of lucky recipients for the last week of the flamingo campaign has been finalized," Sadie said, walking back to join the group.

"I hope my name's not on there," Brad said, a mock-disgusted expression crossing his handsome face. "It's a worthy cause and I support it one hundred percent. But I swear that I'll donate twice if you'll just pass by my place."

Smiling, Abby patted his lean cheek. "Please feel free to donate as much as you wish, but we're making no promises that you won't find the flamingos on your lawn some morning."

Everyone laughed as the group moved into the ballroom, where tables with elegant settings surrounded the hardwood dance floor. A long table had been set up at the front of the room for the current board of officers, and a popular band from Austin had just finished setting up on the bandstand.

When they found their place cards at a table close to the dance floor, Abby was delighted to see that along with the Traverses, she and Brad were seated at the same table with Chris and Macy Richards and Daniel and Elizabeth Warren. All were good friends, and she looked forward to hearing how they planned to spend the holidays.

An hour later, after enjoying a scrumptious prime rib dinner, Abby and the other women excused themselves to go to the powder room to freshen their makeup. When they returned, the band had just started to play a very popular tune, and several couples were making their way to the dance floor.

Draping her shawl over the back of her chair, Abby sat down beside Brad to enjoy watching couples two-step around the dance floor. Dancing in Texas was almost mandatory for every social event, and the fact that there would be dancing before and after the election announcements came as no surprise to Abby.

When the song ended and the band started playing a slow love song, Brad stood and took her hand. "I like the slow ones," he said, leaning close so she could hear him above the band. "I get to hold you."

"Are you sure that's a good idea?" she asked, even as she rose to follow him.

Thus far she hadn't noticed them drawing any undue attention from the ball attendees. But that didn't mean people weren't taking note of the fact that they were together or that they appeared to be a lot more friendly with each other than they had ever been in the past.

"I think it's an excellent idea," he said, pulling her close. "I've been wanting to do this all evening."

She automatically raised her arms to his shoulders as they began to sway in time with the music. "I didn't realize you liked dancing so much."

"I wasn't talking about dancing, darlin'." He gave her a grin that left no doubt what he meant. "I've wanted to hold your body against mine ever since you opened your door when I came to pick you up."

The feel of his hands on her bare skin made her wonder if the backless gown had been the best choice. It reminded her of the night before and having his hands touch her in places she would love for him to be touching her now.

"I can't wait to get you back to my place," he said huskily. "As much as I like seeing you in this slinky black dress, I can't wait to take it off of you."

His impassioned words sent a tingle of excitement straight up her spine. "I don't remember saying I would go home with you."

"But you will," he said. It wasn't a question, and she

was certain Brad believed that she would go along with what he wanted.

Truth to tell, that was exactly what she wanted, too, and that frightened her. Falling asleep in his arms after the most incredible lovemaking she had ever experienced, then waking up with him, had been wonderful. It made her want to do it again and again. For the rest of her life.

Abby bit her lip and forced herself to breathe. What had she done? How could she have let it happen?

She had fought against it, tried to hide from it and denied it was happening. But there was no sense in lying to herself any longer. She had done the unthinkable. She had fallen in love with Brad Price, and it scared her to death. How ironic that she could hold her own in a corporate boardroom, but love terrified her.

What if, like her husband and the baby she was supposed to adopt, Brad was lost to her? It seemed in the past those she loved were taken away from her.

Panic like nothing she had ever known coursed through her. She needed time to think, time to analyze what had happened and why her feelings for Brad were so much more intense than what she had felt for Richard.

As the song ended and Brad led Abby off the dance floor, he noticed that she looked a little shaken. "Are you feeling all right?" he asked.

She stared at him a moment before she finally nodded. "Y-yes. I'm…um, fine."

The sheer panic he saw in the depths of her vibrant

blue eyes had him shaking his head. "I'm not buying it. What's wrong?"

She tried smiling, but it just made her look more unnerved. "I'm just a little…tired," she said, her eyes darting around as if looking for an escape. "That's all."

He had seen her when she was dead on her feet and the expression she wore now wasn't one of fatigue. She looked…desperate?

Frowning, he held her chair as she sat back down at their table, then took his seat beside her. He had no idea what happened to suddenly make her look as if she were trapped, but he was sure as hell going to get to the bottom of whatever was wrong. If she had witnessed anyone at the ball pointing or staring longer than was polite, or if she'd heard a whisper of gossip about them, he personally intended to make whoever it was rue the day they were born.

Unfortunately, Mitch Taylor chose that exact moment to step up to the microphone to address the crowd, preventing Brad from questioning her about who or what had upset her.

"Good evening," Mitch said cheerfully. "I think it's time to announce who will be leading the Texas Cattleman's Club for the next couple of years." He waited for the applause to die down. "Let me start off by saying the vote was a sixty-forty split. That's a lot closer than we've had in several years."

Brad tuned out the rest of what the man was saying as he concentrated on the woman beside him. Abby had to be the most beautiful, alluring woman he had ever known. With her long, dark auburn hair swept up into some kind of twisted knot at the back of her head and the diamond earrings dangling down from her delicate ears, she looked regal, sophisticated and so damned sexy, he had been fighting with himself the entire evening to keep everyone at the ball from learning just how much she made him want her.

Unable to stop himself, Brad reached over to touch the shoulder of her long, black evening dress. Soft and slinky, it hugged her upper body like a second skin, then flared out at her hips to sway with every move she made. That had been enough to drive him half out of his mind. But when he had taken her into his arms to dance, the feel of her bare back beneath his palms had all but sent him over the edge. It brought back the erotic memory of having her in his bed, of touching her satiny skin and feeling her warm from the sizzling heat that he built inside of her.

"...Bradford Price," he heard Mitch say a moment before the room broke out into applause.

Concentrating solely on Abby, it took a moment for Brad to realize that he had won the presidency of the Texas Cattleman's Club. When the news began to sink in, he couldn't help but feel that it was a hollow victory. He had won, but that meant Abby had lost.

"Congratulations," she said, sticking out her hand to shake his.

He ignored the gesture and pulled her into his arms to hold her close. "I'm sorry, darlin'. I know how much you wanted to be the first female president of the TCC."

"Believe me, I'm going to be just fine." Leaning back, she shook her head. "You won fair and square. Now I think you had better get up there and thank everyone for their vote."

He knew she was right. It was expected of the winner to give a victory speech. But at the moment, the last thing he wanted to do was stand up in front of the crowd to thank them for entrusting the club's future to him. He would much rather stay at her side and find out what was bothering her.

As he rose to his feet, he gave her what he hoped was an encouraging smile. "As soon as it's socially acceptable, we're leaving."

"We'll see," she said, as he started toward the podium.

When Mitch presented him with the carved gavel that had called the club to order for over a hundred years, Brad couldn't help but feel humbled as well was honored. "Thank you all for being here tonight and for trusting me to uphold the Leadership, Justice and Peace that this prestigious organization stands for."

As he stared out at the crowd, he realized it was time for the healing to begin—to bridge the gap between the old guard and the new generation of the TCC. "As my first order of business, I'm going to break protocol for a few moments and ask that we take a vote on a handful of issues that I believe will ensure a successful future for the Texas Cattleman's Club and that our esteemed founder would support without hesitation."

He could tell the crowd was intrigued and felt confident in proceeding. "I would like to propose that instead of a new building, we ask Daniel Warren to design an addition that will encompass this clubhouse, merging tradition with modernization. By doing it this way, the existing structure Tex Langley built all those years ago will truly become the heart of our organization."

There was a moment of silence as everyone digested what he was proposing, then to his immense satisfaction the entire room rose to their feet to applaud. Someone shouted that they seconded the motion, enabling the members to vote.

"Will members of the club, please vote by a show of hands?" Brad instructed. "All in favor." There wasn't a single member who didn't have his hand high in the air. Even though Brad knew there were no objections, he had to ask as a rule of order to make the vote official. "Opposed?" When no one responded, he brought the gavel down for the first time as TCC president. "The motion carries by unanimous vote."

"What about the plans for the new building?" someone in the back called out.

"What do you propose we do with them?" another chimed in.

"That's my next order of business," Brad said, smiling. "It has recently been brought to my attention that my sister, Sadie, has plans underway to start a new family center—one that will not only bring cultural exhibits and activities to Royal for families to enjoy together, but also provide assistance and aid for families in crisis. Her plan is for the foundation to work in conjunction with the Helping Hands Women's Shelter over in Somerset. I would like to propose that the design for the new building be donated to the Pruitt Foundation for the purpose of constructing the Tex Langley Cultural Family Center. And to alleviate the problem of where it will be built, I'm donating land that I own at the edge of town, as well as pledging a million dollars toward the construction of the Center."

Before he could even bring it to an official vote, TCC members began calling out pledges for the project. He then went through the procedure to make things official, and by the time he glanced over at the table where Sadie was seated, tears of happiness were streaming down his sister's cheeks.

"Now for my last order of business before I make an official announcement and we get back to celebrating the season, I want to acknowledge the many contributions made over the past year by the women of Royal," he said, knowing he was quite possibly wading into the proverbial swamp filled with alligators. "Without their help and support we wouldn't have found Daniel Warren, the architect whose brilliant designs are going to carry our organization as well as the good town of Royal into the future. I would also like to personally add my heartfelt gratitude to the women—especially Sheila Travers—for the support and caring shown my niece when she was abandoned on the club's doorstep."

To the men's credit, they all rose to their feet to give the women a standing ovation.

"I think we all have to agree that these women have met the standards set forth by our founder, Tex Langley," Brad stated firmly.

He noticed that many of the old guard—the ones most staunchly opposed to admitting female members to the club—were glancing nervously at their wives. Brad almost laughed out loud. Apparently the rumors he had heard of the women withholding certain marital

privileges as a way of protesting their husbands' stalwart stand on the issue were true.

"I would therefore like to propose that after the first
of the year, we take a vote to admit women with all
rights and privileges into the Texas Cattleman's Club,"
he finished.

The thunderous applause that followed was almost
deafening, and by the time they died down, Brad wondered how long it would take for his ears to stop ringing.

Looking over at the table where he and Abby had
been seated, he frowned when he noticed her chair was
empty. Where was she?

Announcing his news about semipro football coming
to Royal and the plans to use the stadium he, Chris
and Zeke were having built for entertainment events as
well as games, Brad ended by wishing everyone happy
holidays. When he stepped away from the podium, it
seemed as if it took forever to make his way through
the crowd of well-wishers over to the table where Sadie
and Rick had been seated.

"Where's Abby?" he demanded, as soon as he
reached them.

Sadie looked worried as she handed him a folded
piece of paper. "She had one of the waiters bring this
for me to give to you." His sister caught her trem-
bling lower lip between her teeth for a moment before
adding, "I think Abby's gone, Brad."

He hadn't looked at the piece of paper and a nag-
ging suspicion deep in his gut told him that he wasn't
going to like the message inside. The last time he had
received a note someone had been trying to blackmail

him, and he had come to think of missives like the one in his hand as bearing nothing but bad news. He stuffed the paper into his pocket without so much as glancing at it.

The word Brad uttered was graphic and one he normally reserved for the guys in the locker room. "I have a feeling I know where she's headed."

His sister's hand on his arm stopped him in his tracks. "Don't follow her if you don't mean it, Brad. Right now she's running from herself more than she is running from you."

"I have to talk to her," he said, feeling desperation begin to claw at his insides. "This could take some time. Will you—"

"Rick and I will go back to your house and relieve Juanita from watching the kids," Sadie said, gathering her evening bag and satin capelet. "We'll stay with Sunnie until you get back."

Rick nodded as he reached into the front pocket of his tuxedo. "Take my Navigator," he said, handing a set of keys to Brad. "She probably had the limo driver take her home. We'll catch a ride with Zeke and Sheila. Good luck, man."

"Thanks, Rick. I owe you one," Brad called over his shoulder, already starting toward the ballroom's emergency exit. The side door was closer to the parking lot, and the way he saw it every second counted.

Quickly finding his brother-in-law's luxury SUV, Brad jumped in behind the steering wheel and, gunning the engine, shot from the parking space. When he reached the street, the tires squealed and left a good amount of rubber on the asphalt as he pressed down on the gas pedal. He had to stop Abby and find out why she was leaving Royal, leaving him.

When he reached the city limits, Brad pushed the accelerator all the way to the floor as he sped down the highway toward her ranch outside of town. He remembered her mentioning the offer from her former associates, but she had told him she wasn't going to accept due to her run for the TCC presidency. Could winning the office have meant more to her than she let on?

He didn't think that was the case. With the announcement that he was the winner, she had almost seemed relieved. Could the loss have made it convenient for her to run from him and what had developed between them?

A sinking feeling began to spread through his chest as he turned the vehicle onto the drive leading up to the Langley ranch. The house was completely dark, and Abby's SUV was gone from where she usually kept it parked. Knowing in his heart it was futile, Brad got out of the truck and walked up onto the porch to try the door anyway. It was locked up tight. Even her housekeeper had left for the evening

Feeling a mixture of anger and pain begin to settle in his chest, he walked back to Rick's SUV and climbed in. She must have left as soon as he got up to give his speech. That meant she had a good half hour's head start on him and most likely had taken the Langley jet back to Seattle. There was no way he could catch her tonight. But if she thought that leaving was the end of things between them, she had another think coming.

For as long as he could remember there had been a tension between them that, up until recently, he hadn't been able to figure out. But in the past several weeks, the feelings had reached a fevered pitch, and now he recognized them for what they were. He had fallen in love with Abby. Hell, he had probably loved her all of his life and had just been too stubborn to realize it.

So what was he going to do about it? What could he do about it with her running away to hide out in Seattle?

Reaching into the inside pocket of his tuxedo jacket, he pulled out his cell phone and called his house. When his sister answered, he didn't mince words.

"Sadie, ask Rick to start calling airlines to get me on the first available nonstop flight to Seattle tomorrow morning while you start packing Sunnie's clothes and whatever else you think I'll need for her."

"How long do you think you'll be gone?" she asked.

"I don't know," he admitted, shaking his head. "But I can tell you this much. We won't be coming back until we bring Abby with us."

Nine

Standing at the floor-to-ceiling window, Abby pulled her bulky sweater close around her as she watched a bald eagle swoop down to scoop up a fish from the waters of Lake Washington. Her jet had landed sometime around dawn and although she had gone to bed as soon as the taxi had dropped her off at her home, sleep had eluded her. She had a feeling that was going to be the case for some time to come.

When she finally gave up trying, she had spent the rest of the day laundering the clothes she had stored at the house and removing the sheets draped over the furniture to keep them from being coated with dust. Once the agency opened, she arranged for a rental car to use until she could have her SUV transported from the Dallas airport. She had managed to keep herself busy enough not to think for the majority of the day, but now that evening was rapidly approaching, Abby found herself with too much time on her hands and nothing to do but think.

Sighing heavily, she turned to walk back into the kitchen for another cup of coffee. She had always loved her house on the water, loved the view that reminded her of the lake just outside of Royal. But now it reminded her only of Brad, of the first time he had kissed her. They had been only six years old at the time, but there had been something in that innocent kiss—some kind of magic—that she feared may very well have branded her for life.

For years, she had attributed the uneasiness, the feeling of being on edge, whenever she was anywhere near Brad to the game of one-upsmanship they had played throughout their lives. He kept her sharp, kept her waiting for a move so that she could make a countermove. Now she knew that all of that had been a veneer, a concealment of the attraction and sexual tension that lay just beneath the surface of their rivalry.

What had taken her so long to figure it out? Why hadn't she been able to see it before now?

Curling up on the couch with her cup of coffee, she closed her eyes as she tried to sort through her tangled emotions. She had loved Richard, and if he hadn't passed away, she had no doubt they would have spent the rest of their lives together. He had been her best friend and confidant, her safe haven. The comfortable companionship they shared more than made up for the lack of passion in their marriage. Abby now recognized that she had married him because he was safe and reliable—a man who she was certain wouldn't have a roving eye and leave her for someone else the way her father had left her mother.

But her relationship with Brad was at the opposite end of the spectrum. They had never been friends in the traditional sense and she doubted they ever would be, doubted it was even possible. He challenged her to go further and achieve more, and there was way too much explosive chemistry between them for their relationship to ever be sedate. The degree of passion and smoldering desire that she had experienced with Brad was unlike anything she had ever known. And God help her, she loved it that way, loved that he made her feel vital and alive. Simply put, she loved him.

But loving him scared her as little else could. What if she lost him the way she'd lost everyone else she cared about?

Looking back, she could see now that it had started with the loss of her father when he abandoned his family. She had been a daddy's girl and was devastated by his betrayal and total lack of contact with her. Then, Richard had been taken from her barely six months after their wedding. She had even lost the baby she had hoped to adopt when the birth mother changed her mind at the last minute.

Shaking her head, she put her cup down. She got up from the couch, went over to open the sliding door and walked out onto the deck. The moon had just begun to rise over the Cascade Mountains in the distance. Its reflection on the dark waters of the lake normally fascinated her, but tonight she barely noticed it.

No matter how much she loved Brad and his adorable baby niece, she couldn't subject herself to that kind of pain again. What would she do when he decided to move on to the next woman he found intriguing? Then where would she be? Or God forbid, what if something happened to one of them?

As difficult as it had been to leave Royal again, she knew in her heart that she had made the right decision. She was much better off in Seattle where she couldn't see them almost daily and wouldn't be reminded of what she could never have. In time, she might even be able to reduce the amount of time she spent wondering about them to once or twice a day.

As she tried to convince herself that was even possible, she heard someone walking along the side deck. Sighing, she waited for them to make their way around to the back. She should have known the solitude she so desperately wanted wouldn't last for very long. Mrs. Norris down the way had been out walking her poodle, Max, when Abby walked back from the market earlier in the evening, and she wasn't at all surprised that the elderly woman had decided to stop by to welcome her back to the neighborhood.

"Mrs. Norris, I'm sorry but I just got back into town and this really isn't a good time," she called out. Hopefully, the woman would take the hint that Abby didn't want to be bothered and give her at least one day to regain what little composure she had left. "Could you please come back in the morning? We'll have coffee and catch up."

"I'm not Mrs. Norris, and no, I'm not going to wait until tomorrow morning," she heard Brad say, as he came around the corner of the house. "You and I are going to have a long talk. Now."

When she turned to face him, Abby's breath caught on a sob. Standing just a few feet away with a baby carrier in one hand, a large duffel bag in the other and a diaper bag slung over his shoulder he had never looked more appealing or more angry.

"W-what are you…" Her voice trembled, and she paused to try to get it back under control. "…doing here, Brad?" She didn't question how he'd found her. He had obviously gotten her address from Sadie.

"Sunnie and I decided to find out why the hell you took off like a thief in the night," he said, setting the duffel bag at his feet. "That was rude of you, darlin'."

A stiff breeze whipped her hair around and she brushed it out of her eyes to point to the house. "Let's go inside. Sunnie doesn't need to be out in this night air." She started to take the baby carrier from him, but his body language held her back.

Walking to the sliding door, her hand shook as she opened it. She stood aside for him to pick up his bag and carry it and the baby inside. When she followed him into her living room, she found the spacious area seemed to have shrunk in size, and she suspected that Brad's presence was the reason.

She had always heard the phrase *larger than life,* but she had never fully understood it until that moment. At the best of times, Brad Price could be imposing. Angry, he was downright intimidating.

As she stood there, wondering what she could say that would get him to leave and let her get back to trying to rebuild her life—a life without him and Sunnie—Brad set the duffel and the diaper bag on the

floor with a thump. The sound seemed to echo throughout the room and emphasized the strained silence.

"Imagine my surprise last night when I stepped
down from the podium to discover that my date for
the evening had ditched me." He set the baby carrier
on the couch, pulled the blanket back and unbuckled
the straps holding the baby safely in the seat. "The least
you could have done was stick around long enough to
say goodbye," he said, lifting Sunnie to his shoulder.
Turning to face her, his hazel gaze seemed to bore all
the way to her soul. "You owed me that much, Abby."

"I-I'm sorry," she said, unable to think of anything
else to say.

The man she loved more than she could have ever
believed possible was standing there holding the baby
she adored and it was breaking her heart. Whatever she
finally settled on saying to him would send them back
to Texas and out of her life for good.

He shook his head. "*Sorry* doesn't cut it with me. I
didn't travel two thousand miles with a baby in tow to
leave here without some damned good answers. You
owe me an explanation for what happened last night
and what sent you running back here."

Sunnie began to whimper and squirm, saving Abby
from having to think of something to say that would
appease him. She knew it was only prolonging the in-
evitable, but maybe it would give her a little time to
think of what she could say that would convince him
that her leaving Royal was for the best.

"Let me take her," Abby said, reaching for the baby.
"I'll change her diaper while you get a bottle ready."

He stared at her a moment before he nodded and

reached for the diaper bag. "We'll wait until we have her down for the night before we resume this conversation. But rest assured, darlin'. We will be having a heart-to-heart talk."

Ten minutes later, Abby sat on the couch, giving Sunnie a bottle while Brad sat in the armchair across from her. Neither had a lot to say, and the tension was almost more than she could bear.

"I'm sure everyone was excited to hear about the football team," she said, unable to stand the silence a moment longer.

"It generated a fair amount of excitement," he said, nodding.

When he didn't say more, she tried again. "What did the membership decide about the clubhouse?"

"They voted to donate Daniel Warren's plans to Sadie's foundation for the purpose of building her cultural center and put on an addition that will encompass the entire existing clubhouse," he answered, his expression as stoic as his voice.

She lifted Sunnie to her shoulder for a burp. "Who made that proposal?"

"I did."

"It's an excellent idea," she said.

He shrugged, but didn't comment further.

As she gave Sunnie the rest of her bottle, Abby felt as if her nerves were going to snap in two. In all of the years she had known him, she had never seen Brad so emotionless, so completely detached. It was as if he was sizing up an adversary, learning her weaknesses in order to use them to his advantage. Knowing she was the opponent he focused on only increased her anxiety.

"Do you think the men will eventually vote to allow more women into the club?" she asked, grasping at anything to keep him talking. If she could get him to open up a bit, then maybe their conversation later would be a little less intense.

"You should have stuck around," he said, his tone lacking even a trace of inflection. "After the first of the year, there will be a vote to admit women to the club. I fully expect it to pass."

"That's wonderful." She was happy to hear that women would finally be admitted to the TCC, but due to the state of her nerves and the fact that Sunnie had gone to sleep, Abby found it hard to work up a lot of enthusiasm.

The time she had dreaded since seeing Brad walk around the corner of her house had come. They were finished with small talk. There was nothing stopping them from the confrontation he was determined they were going to have.

"I'll put Sunnie in her carrier," he said, reaching down to pick up the baby.

Abby jumped. She had been so distracted by the thought of their upcoming conversation, she failed to notice that Brad left the chair and walked over to where she sat.

When he lifted Sunnie from her arms his fingers brushed her breast, sending a bittersweet longing throughout her body. "I—I think I'll make a pot of coffee," she said, suddenly needing to put space between them in order to regain her equilibrium. "If you would like, you can put the baby in my bedroom down the hall."

He nodded. "That's probably a good idea. I don't want our talking to wake her."

Rising to her feet, she showed him the way to the master bedroom. While he set up the baby monitor he had removed from the diaper bag, she went into the kitchen to make coffee. She really didn't think caffeine was a good idea, considering the state of her nerves and his level of tension, but Brad didn't drink anything alcoholic, so offering him wine was out of the question. She reached into the wine rack hanging beneath the cabinet to remove a bottle of chardonnay. He might not need anything stronger than coffee, but she did.

Brad quickly set up the baby monitor, checked to see that Sunnie was sleeping peacefully and walked back into the living room and over to the sliding glass door. Staring out at the lake, he stuffed his hands into the front pockets of his jeans. When his fingers came into contact with the item he had carried with him all the way from Texas, he narrowed his eyes with renewed determination.

"Why did you run, Abby?" he asked, when she walked up behind him. He could tell by her soft gasp that his question startled her.

"I—I don't know what you mean." There was a slight tremor in her voice and he knew she was lying.

"Don't you think it's about time you stop playing your little game and start being honest with both of us?" he asked, turning to face her.

Dear God, she had to be the most beautiful woman he had ever seen. Even with her hair escaping her loose ponytail and wearing baggy sweatpants and a sweater that practically swallowed her, she made him ache to hold her close and love her with every fiber of his being. It was all he could do to keep from walking over to her, taking her in his arms and kissing her until she admitted the reason she fled: because she was scared to death of what they had between them.

"Brad, I think that…my moving back here is…for the best," she said hesitantly.

"What makes you think that?" he asked, pressing for the answer he knew she was trying to avoid.

"I don't belong in Texas anymore," she said, her gaze not quite meeting his.

"Why not?" All he had to do was keep asking the right questions and he knew it was just a matter of time before she broke down and told him the truth. "With the exception of the years between graduating college and getting married, you've always lived in Royal. Don't you like it there?"

"Yes…I mean no…I—"

"Which is it, darlin'?" He took a step toward her. "No, you don't like it there? Or yes, you do?"

She stared at him for a moment before she gave him a jerky nod. "Y-yes, I love Royal. It's home. But it's not where I…belong."

The abject misery he saw clouding her vivid blue eyes almost tore him apart, but he couldn't give up now. He was too close to getting her to admit the real reason she came running back here, and until she did that, she would never be free of the fear that kept her from embracing the future.

"Where *do* you belong, Abby?"

She wore that trapped look again—the one he'd seen

cross her pretty face last night at the Christmas Ball. "I...here. I belong here."

"Liar." He took another step toward her. "You want to know where I think you belong?"

She shook her head until her ponytail swung back and forth. "No."

"I'm going to tell you anyway, darlin'." He took the last step separating them. "You belong right here in my arms," he said, putting them loosely around her.

"No, Brad," she insisted, still shaking her head emphatically.

"Yes, you do, Abby." He brushed a strand of dark auburn hair from her creamy cheek. "Now, don't you think it's time to stop running and admit why you left me at the ball to come back here?"

"Please...don't do this to me, Brad," she pleaded.

The tears welling up in her eyes caused him to feel like the biggest jerk ever to walk on two legs. Placing his finger beneath her chin, he raised her gaze to his and pressed on. "Why, Abby?"

She closed her eyes tight. "B-because I love you and I don't want to take the chance of losing you, too," she said, tears running down her cheeks. "I lose everyone I love. My dad...Richard...the baby. I can't lose anyone else. I just...can't."

"That's all I needed to hear, darlin'," he said, pulling her tightly against him.

He kissed the top of her head and smoothed her hair away from her face as she sobbed against his chest. He hated himself for causing her so much emotional pain, but there hadn't been any other way around it. In order for them to move forward, she had to share the fear with him that was holding her back. He knew that would have never happened without him pushing her for the truth.

When her sobbing ran its course, he cradled her face in his hands. "Darlin', there are no guarantees in life and no promises that there will be a tomorrow. That goes for all of us. But I can assure you of this. There isn't one single minute of one day for as long as I have breath in my body that I won't love you."

"I can't lose anyone else," she said stubbornly. "It hurts too much."

He should have known Abby wouldn't give up until there wasn't any fight left in her. It was one of the things about her that irritated him the most and at the same time made him love her.

"Darlin', I don't think you have any choice in the matter," he said gently. "You love me, don't you?"

To his immense relief there was no hesitation in her response. "Yes. I didn't want to, but I do."

He laughed. That was his Abby—stalwart until the end. "Then you owe it to the three of us to take a chance. Come back home with me, darlin'. Be my wife and Sunnie's mother."

"You want us to get married?"

Nodding, he walked over to take a small velvet box from Sunnie's diaper bag, then removing the diamond solitaire inside, dropped to one knee in front of her. "Will you marry me, Abigail Langley? Will you help me raise Sunnie and any more children we choose to adopt?" He hoped the tears streaming down her face this time were tears of joy.

As he watched her glance at the ring, then turn her

attention back to him, she slowly began to nod her head. "I can't say no. Yes, I'll marry you, Brad. But where did you get this ring?"

"Sunnie and I did a little shopping in downtown Seattle before we came here," he said, loving her more with each passing second.

He slid the ring on the third finger of her left hand, then rose to take her into his arms and give her a kiss that sealed what he knew would be the union of a lifetime. "I've loved you since that day at the lake when we were six years old," he said seriously. "You stole my heart then and never gave it back." Reaching into the front pocket of his jeans, he pulled out the note she had left with Sadie to give to him the night before and pressed it into her hand. "I traveled over two thousand miles to give this back to you, darlin'. I haven't read it and I don't ever intend to."

"Why?" she asked. Her gaze was filled with so much love that it made him feel weak.

"Because I knew it wasn't over for us," he said, kissing her forehead. "You're my soul mate—my other half. Words on a piece of paper could never end that."

Content just to be in each other's arms once again, they remained silent for some time before she leaned back to look up at him. "Are you sure you want me, Brad? I can't have children and won't be able to give you a child of your own."

He used his index finger to smooth away her worried frown. "I want us to adopt Sunnie together," he said, loving her more than he ever thought was humanly possible. "We'll have Sunnie and adopt as many more kids as you want. But I'm not one of those men who thinks that he can't be a dad unless his blood flows through a child's veins."

"I tried to adopt a baby this past summer," she said quietly. "I didn't tell anyone because I was afraid something might happen to stop it."

Her reluctance to talk about her options to become a mother when she first told him about her infertility suddenly made sense. She had tried another way to have the baby she wanted so desperately and it obviously hadn't worked out.

"What prevented the adoption from going through?" he asked, knowing she was ready to talk about it. Otherwise, she wouldn't have brought up the subject.

"When the baby was born, the birth mother changed her mind," she said, her voice filled with sadness. "I went to the hospital to bring my son home and had to leave without him."

So in less than a year Abby had suffered two devastating losses. She had lost a husband as well as the baby she planned to adopt, and there hadn't been a damned thing she could do but stand back and let it happen.

"You don't have to worry about that happening with Sunnie," he said, hoping to find the right words that would reassure her. "Hell, you're already her mother. You've been with her as much as I have. You've changed, fed and put her to bed. You were there to worry over her and help me walk the floor with her when she had the reaction to the immunization. If that doesn't make you her mother, I don't know what does, darlin'."

"I do love her with all my heart," she admitted, smiling.

"Oh, and I guess your loving me is just an after-thought because she and I are a package deal?" he teased.

Her smile warmed him all the way to his soul. "Let's just say I want to keep both of you and leave it at that." Something outside suddenly caught her attention. "Oh, look. It's snowing."

Brad frowned. "Is that unusual?"

She stepped back to take him by the hand. "We don't normally get a lot of snow, but I have something I want you to see."

He willingly followed her out onto the wide deck at the back of the floating home, not sure of what she wanted to show him. When she pointed to the shore across the way, he understood why she liked living on the lake and why it reminded her of the one just outside of Royal.

A dusting of snow covered the hillside and pine trees on the opposite side of Lake Washington, and the lights from the houses made the water look as if diamonds danced on the waves. "It's almost as beautiful as you, darlin'."

"You're only saying that because you love me," she said, wrapping her arms around his waist.

He held her close. "And I'm never going to let you forget it. I'm going to sleep with you in my arms every night and wake up still holding you every morning."

"I love you, Brad."

"And I love you, darlin'. For the rest of our lives."

Epilogue

"Brad, have you seen Sunnie's pacifier?" Abby asked, as they started walking back to the SUV after attending the groundbreaking ceremony for the new Tex Langley Cultural Family Center on New Year's Eve. "She had it in her mouth just a minute ago."

Shaking his head, he reached into the pocket of his suit jacket. "Here's another one." His good-natured laughter made her love him even more. "If our daughter is typical of how often a baby loses these things, then I think I'll buy a few thousand shares of stock in the company that makes them. We'll make a fortune in no time."

Abby smiled at Brad's reference to being Sunnie's daddy. On the return flight from Seattle, they had discussed how they should handle the relationship with the little girl and decided that it would be less confusing for the baby if they referred to her as their daughter. They were going to be raising her as their own and fully intended for her to know that they loved her and wanted to be her parents. Every child needed a mommy and a daddy, and that was exactly what they intended to be for Sunnie.

When he lifted the baby from her arms to secure her in the car seat, Brad's fingers grazed Abby's breast, and even through her coat the sensation sent an exciting thrill skipping up her spine. Their gazes met, and the smoldering promise in his hazel eyes made her feel as if she were the most cherished woman in the world.

"Are you ready to head on over to the clubhouse?" he asked, giving her a quick kiss.

"I've never been more ready for anything in my entire life," she said, meaning every word. "But what about you? You'll be giving up a lot. Are you sure you want to do that?"

He helped her into the passenger seat, then walked around to get in on the driver's side. "You know, I've thought a lot about all the women I dated over the years, and I've come to the conclusion that I was trying to see if one of them could make me feel even a fraction of what I've always felt for you." He lifted her hand and kissed the engagement ring he gave her two weeks earlier. "I can honestly say none of them even came close, darlin'."

"Good answer, Price," she said, grinning.

"It's the truth," he said, starting the truck. Steering her Escalade out onto the road leading across town, he asked, "Did my sister tell you she and Rick are keeping the baby tonight?"

Abby nodded. "Sadie said to bring the baby's things to the ceremony so she and Rick can take Sunnie home with them. That's the extra bag you put in the back before we left the house."

"You do realize we won't be staying long at the reception, don't you?" he asked, the suggestive look in his eyes leaving no doubt what he had planned for later.

As they passed his home on the way to the TCC clubhouse, Abby couldn't help but laugh out loud. "Look, Brad. Your name must have been the last one on the list."

She laughed even harder when he pulled the SUV to a halt in the middle of the road to stare open-mouthed at the hot pink flamingos scattered all over his front lawn. The rare dusting of snow the area had got the night before made the hot pink seem more bright and gaudy than ever.

Restarting the truck, Brad shook his head as he drove on toward the TCC clubhouse. "I don't want to think about a herd of—"

"I think you mean flock," she corrected. "And it could be worse. They could be pink elephants."

"Whatever. We have other things to concentrate on today." Taking her hand in his, he smiled. "Nothing is more important to me than meeting you under the Leadership, Justice and Peace sign in the main ballroom at two o'clock."

Her heart was filled with more love than she could have ever imagined. "I love you more than life itself, Brad Price. I'll be there."

An hour later, as Zeke Travers walked Abby across the ballroom toward the sign that for generations had been a reminder of what the Texas Cattleman's Club stood for, her eyes never left Brad's. He looked so handsome waiting for her in his black tuxedo, a red rosebud pinned to the lapel.

He was the man she loved with all her heart, the man who had made her realize that love was worth more than the risk of losing, and the man who was going to make her dream of having a family of her own come true.

"Are you ready to start the New Year as Mrs. Price?" Brad asked, when she stood facing him beneath the sign.

"I think I've been ready for this all of my life," she said sincerely as they turned to face the minister.

* * * * *

PASSION

For a spicier, decidedly hotter read—
this is your destination for romance!

COMING NEXT MONTH
AVAILABLE JANUARY 10, 2012

#2131 TERMS OF ENGAGEMENT
Ann Major

#2132 SEX, LIES AND THE SOUTHERN BELLE
Dynasties: The Kincaids
Kathie DeNosky

#2133 THE NANNY BOMBSHELL
Billionaires and Babies
Michelle Celmer

#2134 A COWBOY COMES HOME
Colorado Cattle Barons
Barbara Dunlop

#2135 INTO HIS PRIVATE DOMAIN
The Men of Wolff Mountain
Janice Maynard

#2136 A SECRET BIRTHRIGHT
Olivia Gates

You can find more information on upcoming Harlequin® titles,
free excerpts and more at www.HarlequinInsideRomance.com.

HDCNM1211

REQUEST YOUR FREE BOOKS!
2 FREE NOVELS PLUS 2 FREE GIFTS!

Harlequin

Desire

ALWAYS POWERFUL, PASSIONATE AND PROVOCATIVE

YES! Please send me 2 FREE Harlequin Desire® novels and my 2 FREE gifts (gifts are worth about $10). After receiving them, if I don't wish to receive any more books, I can return the shipping statement marked "cancel." If I don't cancel, I will receive 6 brand-new novels every month and be billed just $4.30 per book in the U.S. or $4.99 per book in Canada. That's a saving of at least 14% off the cover price! It's quite a bargain! Shipping and handling is just 50¢ per book in the U.S. and 75¢ per book in Canada.* I understand that accepting the 2 free books and gifts places me under no obligation to buy anything. I can always return a shipment and cancel at any time. Even if I never buy another book, the two free books and gifts are mine to keep forever.

225/326 HDN FEF3

Name	(PLEASE PRINT)	
Address		Apt. #
City	State/Prov.	Zip/Postal Code

Signature (if under 18, a parent or guardian must sign)

Mail to the **Reader Service:**

IN U.S.A.: P.O. Box 1867, Buffalo, NY 14240-1867
IN CANADA: P.O. Box 609, Fort Erie, Ontario L2A 5X3

Not valid for current subscribers to Harlequin Desire books.

Want to try two free books from another line?
Call 1-800-873-8635 or visit www.ReaderService.com.

* Terms and prices subject to change without notice. Prices do not include applicable taxes. Sales tax applicable in N.Y. Canadian residents will be charged applicable taxes. Offer not valid in Quebec. This offer is limited to one order per household. All orders subject to credit approval. Credit or debit balances in a customer's account(s) may be offset by any other outstanding balance owed by or to the customer. Please allow 4 to 6 weeks for delivery. Offer available while quantities last.

Your Privacy—The Reader Service is committed to protecting your privacy. Our Privacy Policy is available online at www.ReaderService.com or upon request from the Reader Service.

We make a portion of our mailing list available to reputable third parties that offer products we believe may interest you. If you prefer that we not exchange your name with third parties, or if you wish to clarify or modify your communication preferences, please visit us at www.ReaderService.com/consumerschoice or write to us at Reader Service Preference Service, P.O. Box 9062, Buffalo, NY 14269. Include your complete name and address.

HDES1

Harlequin *Presents*®

USA TODAY bestselling author

Penny Jordan

brings you her newest romance

PASSION AND THE PRINCE

Prince Marco di Lucchesi can't hide his proud
disdain for fiery English rose Lily Wrightington—
or his attraction to her! While touring the palazzos
of northern Italy, the atmosphere heats up…until
shadows from Lily's past come out….

*Can Marco keep his passion under wraps
enough to protect her, or will it unleash itself, too?*

Find out in January 2012!

*Brittany Grayson survived a horrible ordeal at the hands
of a serial killer known as The Professional...
who's after her now?*

*Harlequin® Romantic Suspense presents a new installment
in Carla Cassidy's reader-favorite miniseries,*
LAWMEN OF BLACK ROCK.

Enjoy a sneak peek of
TOOL BELT DEFENDER.

*Available January 2012
from Harlequin® Romantic Suspense.*

"**B**rittany?" His voice was deep and pleasant and made
her realize she'd been staring at him openmouthed through
the screen door.

"Yes, I'm Brittany and you must be…" Her mind suddenly went blank.

"Alex. Alex Crawford, Chad's friend. You called him
about a deck?"

As she unlocked the screen, she realized she wasn'
quite ready yet to allow a stranger inside, especially a male
stranger.

"Yes, I did. It's nice to meet you, Alex. Let's walk around
back and I'll show you what I have in mind," she said. She
frowned as she realized there was no car in her driveway
"Did you walk here?" she asked.

His eyes were a warm blue that stood out against hi
tanned face and was complemented by his slightly shagg
dark hair. "I live three doors up." He pointed up the street t
the Walker home that had been on the market for a while.

"How long have you lived there?"

"I moved in about six weeks ago," he replied as the

walked around the side of the house.

That explained why she didn't know the Walkers had moved out and Mr. Hard Body had moved in. Six weeks ago she'd still been living at her brother Benjamin's house trying to heal from the trauma she'd lived through.

As they reached the backyard she motioned toward the broken brick patio just outside the back door. "What I'd like is a wooden deck big enough to hold a barbecue pit and an umbrella table and, of course, lots of people."

He nodded and pulled a tape measure from his tool belt. "An outdoor entertainment area," he said.

"Exactly," she replied and watched as he began to walk the site. The last thing Brittany had wanted to think about over the past eight months of her life was men. But looking at Alex Crawford definitely gave her a slight flutter of pure feminine pleasure.

Will Brittany be able to heal in the arms of Alex, her hotter-than-sin handyman...or will a second psychopath silence her forever? Find out in
TOOL BELT DEFENDER
Available January 2012
from Harlequin® Romantic Suspense
wherever books are sold.

SPECIAL EDITION

Life, Love and Family

Karen Templeton

introduces

The FORTUNES *of* TEXAS: Whirlwind Romance

When a tornado destroys Red Rock, Texas,
Christina Hastings finds herself trapped in the
rubble with telecommunications heir
Scott Fortune. He's handsome, smart and
everything Christina has learned to guard herself
against. As they await rescue, an unlikely attraction
forms between the two and Scott soon finds
himself wanting to know about this mysterious
beauty. But can he catch Christina before she runs
away from her true feelings?

FORTUNE'S CINDERELLA

Available December 27th wherever books are sold!

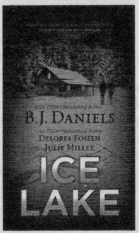